OAKLAND PUBLIC LIBRARY
15 CHURCH STREET
OAKLAND, ME 04963

HONEY BEA

OAKLAND PUBLIC LIBRARY
18 CHURCH STREET
OAKLAND, ME 04963

HONEY BEA

KIM L. SIEGELSON

OAKLAND PUBLIC LIBRARY
8 CHURCH STREET
OAKLAND, ME 04963

JUMP AT THE SUN

HYPERION BOOKS FOR CHILDREN

NEW YORK

5/5/07

Text copyright © 2006 by Kim L. Siegelson
All rights reserved. No part of this book may be reproduced or transmitted in any
form or by any means, electronic or mechanical, including
photocopying, recording, or by any information or storage retrieval system, without
written permission from the publisher. For information address
Hyperion Books for Children, 114 Fifth Avenue,
New York, New York 10011-5690.
Printed in the United States of America
First Edition
1 3 5 7 9 10 8 6 4 2
This book is set in 14-point Centaur MT.
Reinforced binding
Library of Congress Cataloging-in-Publication Data on file.
ISBN 0-7868-0853-5
www.hyperionbooksforchildren.com

For Jenifer,
because I wish *only* blessings for you, my friend.

※ ※ ※

nce in the by'm by, a colony of honeybees lived on the land of a beekeeper. They knew no life besides harvesting nectar from his trees and fields and turning it into sweet, brown honey. Though the beekeeper did no work, he took a large share of their honey every year to sell at market. Seemed to the bees he took more and ever more honey from them so they had less and ever less to eat come wintertime. They complained one to another but saw no way to change things, for he was big and powerful, and they were not.

One year the sun shone just enough, and the rain fell just enough to make the orchards and fields brim with flowers. The honeybees worked hard and harvested more nectar than any time in memory. This will make the beekeeper happy, they thought. There is more than enough for everyone. But the beekeeper knew nothing of fairness. He built a big, new hive and ordered them to fill it, too. And he took so much honey that the bees knew they would surely starve. Some gathered together and decided to leave the beekeeper's land. They took wing. Soon, others followed. Every day another few flew away until the hives finally emptied.

The beekeeper couldn't harvest the nectar, and so he had nothing to sell at market. Not one drop of sweet, brown honey. And when winter frosts came round, 'twas him *who nearly starved.*

—a story told by Abeille

CHAPTER ONE

Abeille

LD ABEILLE stood chewing a lump of honeycomb at the open door of the slave cabin where she lived. After she'd worked all the sweet from the comb, she spat the wax into one hand and rolled it between her palms. She gazed out at the *jardin de fleurs* that lay to the sunny side of her master's grande maison. The house's thick marble columns glowed rosy-pink in the light of sunset, and the tall glass windows shimmered gold. It was late, but honeybees still hovered among the rose blossoms in the garden, gathering nectar. Always busy gathering.

Abeille had long tended the master's garden, and in all that time he'd not once walked the paths nor stopped to admire a bloom. Even in the heat of summer Reynard Rillieux shut his windows against the perfume that hung in the air like a lady's shawl. But then, a master such as Michie Reynard could do whatever fine or foolish thing he wanted. He owned most of the land in the parish west of Old Devil River: fields and fields of sugarcane for as far as the eye could see, and the largest sugar mill in south Louisián, and several hundred slaves to toil for him.

Those who worked the farm—Abeille included—owned little or nothing, not even themselves. She dropped the mouth-warmed ball of beeswax into a cloth pouch that hung at her waist. Michie could have his endless rows of cane; the garden suited her better. The bees and the flowers knew to whom they truly belonged, and who belonged among them. "A chicken knows which nest box is its own," she told herself.

She had lived for a short time inside the grande maison in a room on the bottom floor, windowless and dark as a cockroach's lair. Michie had given her to his young bride, Mamzelle Rosabel, as a wedding gift. Abeille was to have been a lady's maid, but ended up as nursemaid to the poor girl, barely of the age to wear her hair twisted high in a chignon, much less marry a grown man. Mamzelle cried tears enough to swell the river past its banks and fill the irrigation ditches. Wept herself sick over having to leave her *maman* and her home in France.

Unlike the *jardin de fleurs* planted beneath her bedroom window, Mamzelle did not thrive. The ribbon cane had come from some foreign land, too, but it took to the black silt of Louisián like a true native, ranked thick on every side of the maison and the row of wood-slatted slave cabins and outbuildings behind it. Stalks so tall each tasseled tip appeared to brush the underbellies of drifting clouds. The wind sent it rippling like deep water, like the sea that might surround an island, dusty leaves a-shiver with the sound of hissing snakes.

Abeille turned back into the cabin. Her niece Ara lay abed, laboring hard to birth her first child. She'd been at it for long hours, nearly a full day, and Abeille feared for her and the infant. Such cobwebs of worry hung in the rafters of every birthing room, for birthing was dangerous work for a woman. Some died pushing new life into the world; some took their babes with them. But a failed birth—a stillborn child—brought a worse fate: that a woman be judged as hexed and sold quickly before her bad luck spread to other wombs.

"The worst will soon be over, *cher*," Abeille said, touching the backs of her fingers to Ara's damp forehead. She placed a dish of water on the mantel beside a blue-tinged chicken egg, and lit a beeswax candle. When the scent of honey sweetened the air, she called out for Papa Legbo to open the gate to the spirit world and then spoke a prayer. Not a church prayer, but something more ancient—brought from Afrik:

> *Mary, Ayida-Wedo, Mother of all,*
> *Who knows the struggle and pain of birth,*
> *Ease this woman's labors,*
> *And deliver from her a healthy child.*

Afterward she could do no more but take a seat at Ara's side and wait while the candle burned away, letting her gnarled fingers work patiently over a strand of wooden prayer beads.

Outside, Mawu, the moon, was on the wane; less than half of her full self and giving forth a faded, tepid light. Soon, though, Mawu would wax again and push aside the night with silver brilliance. This was a promise she fulfilled over and over again, and Abeille clung to that one hope as Ara struggled to release the child from her womb.

From somewhere in the shadows a rain owl called from the branches of a live oak. They were birds of wisdom and prophecy, messengers of Mawu, but sometimes omens of death or sickness. Abeille pinched each bead on her string a bit harder while she continued to pray, her eyes open and unblinking. The strange words rolled from her tongue, urgent and pulsing. Soon Ara's labor matched the rhythm.

A baby boy slipped free feet first, arms trailing overhead in a gesture of surrender. He was tiny, gray as ash, and still. Pulled from her trance, Abeille quickly cleared his small mouth with her finger, and sucked the clots from his nose and spat them on the floor. She turned him over and rubbed his back with a tatter cloth, but he would not take breath.

All the while Ara's pain gripped her ever more fiercely, until, with the last of her strength, she delivered another child, this one a girl, who balled her fists and arched her back at the sudden rush of cool air on her skin. Abeille quickly cut through the belly cord that bound the baby to Ara. "You've a daughter and I've a new grandniece," she said, relieved that the child seemed vigorous. "Born the first day of the harvest season, too."

Ara pushed herself up from the moss-stuffed mattress. "Two were born: *marasa*—twins like you and my *maman*."

"The first never tasted the air, but this one looks ripe, eh?" Abeille leaned close to place the girl in Ara's arms. Her niece might've tossed the baby into the air had Abeille not kept a firm hold.

"She has the veil!" Ara whispered, grimacing.

"*Oui*, she does," Abeille answered soothingly, "just as all the women in our family have for many generations. Only you, her mother, can lift it as symbol of gifts passing from one to the next."

"Curse, not gift," Ara shot back. She stared down at her daughter and trembled. A thin skin covered the baby's face from forelock to narrow chin. Her large, moist eyes stared up through the mask of fine vessels that looked like voile, the sheer cloth used to make veils on ladies' hats. The baby's mouth moved as a fish's does when taken out of water. She began to thrash and fight to breathe.

Ara touched the veil with her fingertips, then drew back. "If I leave the veil over her face, Tante, then will I be allowed to keep my powers?"

"*Non!* There is no going back now, *cher*. Your lifeblood has passed most of its power over to her. The soul she and her twin would have shared belongs only to her, so the power is whole and very strong. All will be lost if you let her die. What if she is the one to become a great priestess—a *mambo* like none since Afrik? Mawu cannot be on the wane forever. There is a prophecy. . . ."

"A lie! A false hope!" Ara snapped, her voice bitter. "This girl will be a slave, Tante, a slave the same as me and you and everyone in the quarter. And she will grow up hated and feared and called witch, Tante, just as we are."

Abeille brought her hand up as if to slap Ara. 'Twas reckless to speak the makings of a curse aloud over a newly born baby; Ara knew this. But rather than strike her niece, Abeille passed her raised hand over the child, drawing symbols of protection in the air with her fingers. Her patience was gone. When she spoke, her voice was harsh and commanding. "Do not end our line by letting this child die tonight! You will lift the veil or suffer my anger all your remaining days!"

Ara flinched. She took a single, shuddering breath and tore the membrane. Released, the baby wailed long and loud, and Ara with her. Abeille sank beside them and enfolded her niece in her arms.

"Michie Reynard will want to see her," Ara whispered once the baby had quieted. "He'll want to weigh and measure her, and ink her name in his books."

"*Oui*, he will," Abeille answered. "Tomorrow will be soon enough for that. For today she'll belong only to you. Nurse her while I ready her twin for burial."

"Let me see it. Was it another girl?"

"Boy-child. Small as a kitten and weak as one, too. He'd have been sent to the cane fields in his fifth year and not survived it. The sickly ones don't. Death can be a blessing, *cher*."

Ara turned away and put the baby girl to her breast while Abeille performed the rituals to fix the tiny boy in his grave, for his spirit needed to be sent home to Afrik quickly or it would become jealous of the one who lived.

Abeille lit a new candle and shook a rattle over the boy, then bathed him in water steeped with witch hazel twigs and herbs. She drew a cross on his forehead with a floured finger before wrapping him in a clean white cloth. At last she put him on the bed beside Ara.

Ara couldn't look at him. She felt heavy as stone, her chest hollow as a rotted oak stump. The two babies had emptied her, taken the last sparks of life left in her body, their kicks against her ribs a reminder that she hadn't died in the river with their father. Now she felt hopeless with loss, mortally wounded, as if a cane knife had been pushed into her chest. And she felt the last drops of her magiic ebbing away with every beat of her heart, and every drop of milk that her daughter took from her.

Once Tante Abeille had gone, Ara poured a dipper of water into a washbasin and kneeled over it, waiting for it to grow still. She stared at the reflection of her own face, then deeper, pushing her mind out quickly toward the murkiness of days to come. She found she could not go far, tired as she was from laboring, and tethered too tight to what was now. The baby girl had done this to her—maybe to the boy twin, too. Drained them both of sap. Nothing left now but dry pulp. Fodder for goats, tinder for fire.

The thought chilled her.

Since the age of thirteen she'd been able to swim through Time like it was cold, clear water.

Water lit by sunshine bright enough to help her see into the deepest nooks. She could breathe it easy as any fishtailed siren born to the sea. But now Time felt as tepid and stagnant as a slough. Airless. Thick, muddy clouds swirled up from the bottom to blur her vision almost to blindness.

Even without her eyes she understood well enough what her future would bring. She smelled and felt and tasted what she couldn't see. There would be smoke and salt on her lips, and terrible heartbreak. Pain sharper than a needle's prick, deeper than the ache of childbirth.

A dusting of fresh-turned soil clung to Abeille's skirt hem when she returned. Careful not to bring burial dirt inside the house, she brushed herself off in the yard and poured a ladleful of water over her hands and feet to wash them. She could hear the baby wailing, even though the cabin door and shutters were closed. The birth of Ara's daughter wouldn't be a secret for long, though there'd be none stopping by to offer the usual blessings and help given to new mothers.

Ara was right that the others in the quarter hated them. Blamed them for any bad luck that came. Said they talked to the dead, and knew *wanga* hexes, and could steal your soul if they wanted it. "Them witch-women will fix you with their stink eye!" parents told children. "Walk past fast as you can."

Abeille heard them, but didn't hurt over it like Ara did. The others were fools who couldn't see they conjured their own bad luck by not honoring the *loa* properly. Ancestor spirits grew angry if you ignored them, and didn't perform the rituals.

Inside the cabin she found the baby lying alone on Ara's bed, freshly bathed and swaddled. Ara's dress and head wrap hung on a wall peg near the window. Why would she leave the cabin bareheaded and barely dressed? New worry sifted through Abeille, but she pinched it back. Ara had only gone to the privy. She'd not be away for long.

Abeille knotted an old shawl at one shoulder so that it made a sling, and tucked the baby inside it. She needed to strip Ara's bed to the ropes in order to boil the soiled linens and air the mattress. A broken locket strung on a silver chain lay at the center of the bed. The locket had belonged to Ara's mother, but the face of it had been lost. Ara hadn't taken the chain from her neck since the day Abeille clasped it around her throat and told her it was a talisman—perhaps an important connection to her mother. Yet here it was, left behind with the baby.

Fear squeezed Abeille's chest. Her niece had been thin-spirited ever since word had come that the river had swallowed her man, confirming what she'd already known. Grief had gnawed at her till she scarcely kept herself alive. She took in only enough food to keep her heart beating and the new life growing in her. Abeille had hoped that mothering a child would bring her to her senses.

Now she cursed herself for leaving Ara so

quickly after the birth. But she'd had no choice: the little boy had to be buried before dawn or death would take another—his twin, or his mother, or his old tante—and Abeille wasn't ready to cross over yet. Too much left undone on this side of life.

And it was best that no one in the quarter learn of the stillbirth. Ara worried enough about what the others thought without that added to it.

Abeille wished for a moment that she'd been given the gift of vision so that she could search for and find where Ara had got to. But her own talent was linked to earth and those things that grew and crawled upon it. Finders and seers were water-linked. Ara had inherited that talent from Abeille's sister-twin. A soul linked to water was drawn to it as a moth to flame, the same way the land and its creatures drew her.

"Water . . ." she whispered. Ara had gone to the river. Even without the seer's gift, Abeille knew it was so.

Pale light tinted the sky dishwater-gray and the

cock crowed once as she hastened up the dirt path toward the garden beside the grande maison. A few folks who'd risen early glanced up as she made her way past their doors with the crying newborn baby. She smelled the flowers before she reached the garden gate: jessamine, oleander, lily, and rose. Honeybees hovered and dipped among the blossoms, but she did not stop to greet them in her usual custom.

She breathed heavily as she trotted toward the cookhouse. Abeille stopped to catch her breath and comfort the baby who wailed at being jostled so. Old Las and Perte peered out of the cookhouse, their shoulders touching in the doorway. Las worked as the laundress, and had for so blessed long that her back was bent crooked as an ancient catalpa tree, as though she always carried a basket of wet linen. Old Perte had charge of the cookhouse. Her eyes were milky with age, but she could cook well enough by feel and smell. And Las, with her good eyes, helped.

Las raised her hand and called out, "*Bonjou,* Abeille!"

Abeille raised her hand in return. Among those who worked for Michie Reynard, only Las and Perte treated her with kindness. Abeille went to them and put the infant in Las's gnarled hands. "Ara's daughter," she said.

What questions the old women had, they kept to themselves. At least for the moment. "I'll set a pot of milk to warm beside the hearth," Perte announced. "The little one can suck it from a cloth."

"*Merci,*" Abeille thanked them. "Let me find her mother before it's too late."

CHAPTER TWO

Ara

ARA STOOD atop the earthen levee. The river coursed below her, dark and rippled as a sheet of hammered metal. Watching it made her feel faint; made her sway like a blade of windblown grass. She took a deep breath in the hopes it might clear her mind. But it didn't. The river pulled at her. A voice called out—the voice of her children's father.

He'd tried to run off, even though she'd begged him to wait, just until she gave birth. Then they'd go with him—wherever he wanted. But he wouldn't listen to anyone but the lamed blacksmith from Ayti, the only slave she knew who claimed to have a last name: Gú. Like the blacksmith, her husband wanted freedom more than anything else, and said he could move faster alone.

"Where will you go?" she'd asked, trying not to let her fear show.

"Monsieur Gú says follow north along the river for as far as it goes." He drew his face close to hers and held her gaze for a long time, his eyes serious. "When I'm settled I'll send for you," he promised.

"We will be waiting," she promised in return, knowing the wait would be far too long and hard to bear.

That night she traveled with him for a little while by using her mind's eye and the seer's vision that was her gift. She saw him work his way north along the levee before he made his way down to the river's edge. His bare feet slipped on the muddy bank, his fingers and toes clawing at roots and weeds until he found a sandbar that appeared to reach from one side of the water to the other at a narrow place in the river.

He walked across the spit of sand careful as a man walking a rail fence. The shallows reached knee deep, then waist deep, then to his shoulders, and neck. When his chin touched water, he was more than halfway across. Almost there. Another step, and suddenly the sand collapsed beneath him. A current caught his legs before he could regain footing, and the bottom dropped away beneath him. He struggled against the river, to keep his head above it; fought as the current swept him along and toward the bottom, where he caught in a tangle of sunken trees. His chest burned with the need to breathe. He gulped and coughed, gulped again, and then grew quiet. His clothes billowed about him, and his arms drifted loose at his sides, moving with the water like riverweeds.

Maybe he'd died looking up toward the sky through the murky water; Ara didn't know. Her link to him snapped when his life ended.

Until now. Now he called to her from the river, and how very long she had waited for him to send for her! She strained to hear it more clearly, but another voice intruded: Abeille's voice.

"Stop, niece!" she cried, breathless from running.

Quickly, Ara plunged forward and slid down the grassy side of the levee toward the riverbank. There was no sandbar to cross, but it didn't matter. The river would embrace her; it would take her to her beloved and they would never again be apart. And they would be free. Tante Abeille couldn't understand; she'd never lost her heart to a man. Said love of a man only weakened a woman.

Driftwood barred Ara's path to the riverbank: whole trees piled higher than her head, stripped of bark and sun-bleached till they looked like the gray bones of giants. Heedless, she pushed into the tangle. Sharp branches cut her arms and legs, grabbed her hair, snatched at her slip. Quickly she shucked the slip off and clambered through naked.

Abeille reached the top of the levee above her. Downriver, a man in a boat shouted. Ara made herself deaf to them both. When she reached the water she did not hesitate, but threw herself forward with arms stretched out in greeting.

The river swallowed her.

Its strength and swiftness surprised her, as did the sudden cold that took her breath. It should have panicked her, but she felt nothing except calm relief. Tumbling beneath the surface, she heard more shouts, muffled and distant. Her hip slammed against a stone and sent her spinning. She gulped water. Her lungs felt like fire. Something snagged her hair, and she reached out to push away from it. Her fingers grasped flesh—a man's thick wrist and hand. His grip on her hair tightened and then jerked her upward. She hadn't strength left to fight him, much as she wanted to. He hauled her over the side of his rowboat as if she were a catfish on a line. Lying at his feet, shivering and retching up water, she wept and wept.

The river hadn't kept her. It had betrayed her like everything else.

Abeille stood outside the smokehouse with the babe in her arms. A rusty lock held the door latch in place. There were no windows to look through; she pressed an ear to the door and whispered, "Ara? You awake?"

Her niece answered with a stranger's voice: dull, weary, lifeless. "Overseer says I'll be sent to market come morning . . ." A wet, violent cough cut her words short.

Abeille rattled the lock, but it wouldn't budge. She had no power over such objects, only those that sprouted or crept. "I shouldn't have left you alone," she said. "Overseer should've lashed me instead of you, damn him."

Fifty raw stripes welted the skin of Ara's back and thighs. She coughed again. "I used the last of my magiic to catch sight of my future, Tante. You couldn't have stopped this. No one could."

"You could've let me try, Ara! I might've helped you the way I did your *maman*. Visions are only wet clay. Sometimes we can pinch or push a bit to shape our fate. But now it's hard set, this can't be changed. Nothing to be done."

Ara's fingers slid through a gap between door and frame, and Abeille bent to kiss them. They smelled of smoke and tasted of the salt-cured meat that hung from hooks in the smokehouse rafters.

"Work a charm for me," Ara said. Her voice was brittle, shrill. "Fix Michie. Lay a soul spell on him. Call a *baka* or *diab* and let him be eaten until he is hollow and mute."

Abeille shifted the baby and pushed her own fingers into the gap. "Call evil spirits to make *wanga?*" She didn't say what they both knew: all magiic had a price, some unforeseen *tock* that followed magiic's *tick*. But black magiic extracted the highest price of all, and could even turn around on the practitioner. No such thing as digging in a graveyard without dirtying your hands.

But her heart broke for Ara. She had failed her niece, so how could she deny her one last wish?

Abeille took a thimble from her pouch and pushed it through the gap. "Sing the *Marasa* hymn to your daughter. Bring it straight from your heart. Catch any tears you shed in this."

Ara took it and began to sing for her baby girl and for her buried son the song usually reserved for fêtes in honor of the dead. Her voice trembled:

> Marasa élo, *I have no mother to speak for me.*
> Marasa élo, *I have left her in another land.*
> Marasa élo, *I left my family in Vilokan.*
> Marasa élo, *there is no one now to speak for me.*

When she finished, Abeille passed her a lump of beeswax to seal it. With that done, Ara passed the thimble back to Abeille and said, "Be my daughter's godmother. Protect her."

"*Oui,*" Abeille promised with heavy heart. "You must name her. I will tell Michie, when he asks."

Ara tried to think of something lovely, something that rolled off the tongue, something not tinted with sorrow. "Beatrice," she answered after a moment, knowing how Abeille loved the honeybees in the garden. "I left my mother's locket on the bed," she added. "Give it to Beatrice when she is old enough."

Abeille said nothing. Her voice felt trapped inside her throat, but she touched her mouth to Ara's fingers in answer. Salt mixed with wood ash met her lips. It stung them like nettles.

She pressed the wax more firmly onto the thimble's mouth to seal the tears inside, then licked the bitter grit away from her mouth as she toted Beatrice up the path.

High-stacked clouds had settled in overhead, rosy-gray as the feathered breasts of mourning doves. A wind, smelling of silt and of rain, rattled the cane like dry bones and flailed Abeille's skirt against her legs. She entered the cookhouse where Perte and Las were readying a tray with Michie's coffee. Neither spoke until Abeille said, "She's named the girl Beatrice."

Las stopped her work and came forward to rest a rough palm on the baby's head to bless her.

> *"May your back grow strong from head to hip,*
> *And never feel the master's whip, Beatrice."*

It was a good blessing to give to anyone who worked for Michie Reynard.

Perte placed her hands on Beatrice's chest, and spoke her blessing:

> *"May you grow in beauty and in grace,*
> *More so your heart than limb or face, Beatrice."*

A good blessing to give any child, thought Abeille. In silence she added a final blessing:

Mawu smile upon you;
the loa *protect you from harm, my Beatrice.*

A hush fell again over the three old women as they grieved for Ara. Abeille felt for the thimble inside her pocket. The *wanga* must be started while the tears were fresh with Ara's sorrow. No time to wallow in their own useless tears.

"Let me take Michie his coffee," she offered. "I'll see if I can reason with him to let Ara stay. Law says a mother can't be parted from her child until its tenth year."

"The laws are whatever he decides they are," Perte said, "but you can try."

While Perte added boiling water and grounds to the coffee pot, Abeille took a cup and saucer from the shelf and set them on the cookhouse table. She slipped the thimble from her apron pocket and held it in her hands until it warmed, then whispered into her fist:

"*Crick for crack, and hurt for hurt;*
Come baka, *come* diab, *to feast and work.*"

Then, stripping the beeswax cap away, she tipped Ara's tears into the bottom of the cup and dropped the thimble back in her pocket. If and when the fix worked, it would take its toll on Reynard, and maybe herself. Magiic gathered the world to you for a moment, and the world changed by being gathered. Like a stone dropped into water, one could control the stone but not the ripples caused by dropping it. And didn't ripples always find their way back to the shore from where the stone was first cast?

So be it, Abeille told herself and whatever *loa* spirits were listening. She placed the cup on a silver tray along with the pot of coffee. Before she took it inside the maison, she stopped to pick a white rose from the garden and rested it beside the dish of sugar lumps.

She stepped into the shaded overhang beneath

the upper gallery and entered the maison, musty and quieter than she remembered it. Carefully she placed the tray atop a small table in the corner of the library and waited for him to look up and speak to her.

He's grown old, she thought. See how his hair has turned gray as gunmetal. His hands are ropy with veins, and so spotted that they look like old pink toads.

"You may go," he said finally glancing up from the piles of papers and charts and books lying atop his desk. His eyes narrowed as he took her in. Still clear and sharp as green glass, Abeille observed, a harder version of Ara's. She wondered if he'd ever noticed. He seemed not to remember what had happened the year after Rosabel's death. Where his comfort had come from. She herself never forgot, nor ever forgave herself for helping him.

When Abeille didn't move, Reynard's mouth twisted into a frown, and he peered at her over the lenses of his spectacles. "Why do you stand there staring at me? I've told you to go."

"You've locked my niece in your smokehouse and plan to sell her," Abeille answered, straightening her back a bit. "She has an infant. Even I know there is a law against separating them so early."

He pushed himself from his desk and came toward her. "There is no law to protect a woman who cannot be trusted, who nearly drowned herself trying to escape. Next time she might take the baby with her."

Abeille flinched. "She wouldn't."

"Because she will never have the chance." Reynard took his glasses from the bridge of his nose. Two angry red splotches burned in the hollows of his cheeks. "And if you forget your place again, old crone, you will join her on the stump at auction. Though I doubt there'd be a single bid for the likes of you. I'd give you away just to be rid of you."

Abeille dropped her eyes to the floor, but she could not stop the odor that boiled up from her skin, cider vinegar and sweet almond—the smell of an angry beehive. She struggled to control the vibrant hate in her voice, and to make herself humble. "If you won't keep Ara, then let her child stay with me. Let me raise the girl."

"Healthy?"

"*Oui.* Named Beatrice." Abeille's hand shook, but she managed to lift the pot and pour a steady stream of coffee into the salty puddle of tears at the bottom of the cup. A tendril of steam twined up toward the ceiling and broke apart, and she wondered if such a tiny scrap of vapor could find its way outside and make the long journey up to join the clouds clinging to heaven's skirt hem.

Reynard pinched the cup handle between finger and thumb and took a sip. "Too strong," he muttered, wincing at the taste. "Bitter."

Taking a lump of sugar from the tray, he noticed the rose. A honeybee crawled from inside the folded center petals, changed its mind and turned back. Quickly he flung the bloom to the floor, crushed it and kicked it beneath his desk.

Abeille knew better than to bring flowers inside. She'd seen what a bee sting could do to him, make his eyes swell closed and his tongue fill with blood. He never would have put flowers so close to the house if not for Rosabel and her begging to have something other than cane to gaze out at. He'd have done almost anything to stop that endless weeping—anything but let her leave him.

Abeille bent to gather the scattered petals beneath his desk, smiling when he couldn't see her. She sprinkled the floor with a good measure of dirt taken from the head of the baby boy's grave. Fresh graveyard dirt gave *wanga* greater power.

When she emerged on hands and knees, Reynard grinned down at her in triumph. He took a long draft of coffee and wiped his mustache with the back of his hand, then swirled the coffee grounds in the bottom of the cup three times. "Some believe the future can be seen in dregs such as these." He turned it rim down onto the saucer and held it out to her. A spot of red marked the handle where his fingers had held it, blood drawn by a thorn from the dashed rose.

Abeille knew better than to take the cup from him. He was mocking her, prodding her to anger. She couldn't read futures in the dregs of coffee or tea, nor cards, nor anything else. He knew Derora, her sister, had had an inner eye that saw horizons far ahead. But he didn't know everything: that Ara at birth had inherited the inner eye from Derora. At least Derora had had sense enough to keep some secrets from him, if nothing else, and he'd not had the sense to figure it out for himself.

But what Derora had shared with him cost her dearly in the end, though Abeille rightfully took half the blame. Now Ara was lost, too.

Abeille wondered if she'd done everything wrong in the raising of her sister's daughter. Certainly she'd told Ara about her gift far too early. Rather than prepare the girl, it had made her anxious. She had asked questions Abeille couldn't answer, questions only a seer like Derora could.

When was a dream just a dream, and not a vision? Could visions be turned on and off like the water tap on the cistern? Which insights should a seer pay heed to, and which could she ignore? Did visions always come true?

Abeille didn't know.

She'd coddled Ara out of guilt, demanded little and tolerated much. As payment, her niece hadn't learned to master her gift, and so it had quickly mastered her. She used it without understanding, with little thought of the price it might levy. She steered it poorly, and so it carried her down ever narrower, more twisted paths. "Can't I refuse the gift if I don't want it anymore, Tante?" she'd once asked after a terrible headache followed by nightmares. Her voice had been small and pleading.

Shocked, Abeille had answered in anger. "Never! No more than you can refuse your own blood! No more than you can refuse your skin or your bones! Such a terrible, foolish thing to ask!" At that precise moment a window had closed between them. Abeille could see Ara through it, but could not reach her. Neither of them truly heard the other ever again.

Abeille sighed and bowed her head. It would be different with Beatrice. By Mawu and all the *loa* who heard her, Abeille vowed to make certain of that. She would find the right time to tell the girl of her birthright. She'd steer her with a firm hand. And if she had to, she'd bring Derora back from the grave. *Let me live long enough,* she prayed. *Whatever price I must pay for fixing the old man, let it wait.*

Thinking Abeille's bowed head signaled defeat, Reynard placed his cup on the tray and shoved it toward her. "You may raise the child," he said. Both he and Abeille realized he had no other choice if he wanted the infant to survive. No other woman in the quarter would take the child willingly, and if forced, would likely let her waste away, or smother her in her sleep, or leave her outside to catch her death. No one but Abeille could be trusted to protect the baby.

"If she's to thrive, she'll need mother's milk for a month or two," Abeille said.

Reynard nodded in agreement. "There's a woman in the quarter who birthed a boy not long ago. She can suckle the baby alongside hers. I'll have the overseer tell her."

Abeille set Reynard's tray on the old plank table in the cookhouse, and lifted his cup from the saucer. *Some believe the future can be seen in dregs such as these,* he'd said. She squinted, trying to make sense of the patterns that had formed in the tiny flecks of ground coffee at the bottom, but they said nothing at all to her. "Perte, when you had your eyes, could you see the days-to-come by looking at coffee grounds?"

Perte held Beatrice in the crook of one arm. She dipped the corner of a clean cotton rag into a bowl of sweetened milk and let the baby suck it dry, then dipped again. "It's the making of tonics and tinctures I know. Las can read fortunes."

Neither Perte nor Las had been born with the

veil. What magiic or talent they possessed hadn't been passed along by mother's blood, Abeille knew. An elder woman had taught them root cures and charms, how to read symbols, or find meaning in patterns—the sort of folk magiic called hoodoo. It could be forgotten or put aside, but blood magiic took you when the time came and released you only in favor of a new vessel. There was no escaping it. Still, mightn't folk magiic be a true power, important in its own way? Sometimes it was good to dip bread into another pot.

Las stared at the puddle of coffee in the saucer for a while. "I see a triangle, and inside it a little thimble shape. Triangles point to things unexpected," she said. "The thimble is a sign of change."

"What sort?" Abeille asked.

"That's something I can't know," Las answered.

Perte groaned as she lifted her wide hips off her chair. Abeille took Beatrice from her and bent to kiss the sweet crease of the baby girl's neck. It smelled of milk and honey.

CHAPTER THREE

Beatrice

SEASON followed season until twelve years passed by. Certainly Beatrice didn't feel the rush of years in the same way her old tantes did. Time drew her up inch by inch even as it weighed heavily on them. Tante Perte grew blinder, and Tante Las more stooped. Tante Abeille changed the least, with only a little more gray in her hair to show time's passage. It was she who told Beatrice that she was twelve years old on the first day of the cane harvest. The air smelled green that day, and a little of souring pulp.

Before they'd eaten their breakfast of bread and honey, Tante's exact words to her were, "You are coming into yourself now, *piti*. Tell me, have you felt the waxing of the moon yet?"

"*Non*, Tante," she'd answered, thinking Tante wanted to know if she'd had her first moon cycle. Tante Perte and Tante Las had explained what would happen, and she didn't need to talk about it yet again with Tante Abeille. Most especially not with her, because surely there would be some sort of ceremony to celebrate the occasion just as there'd been when she'd lost her last baby tooth: a long night of song and dance; the burning of candles; the drawing of *vevers*—magical names of *loa* spirits—on the ground, with white flour and black ash.

Who but Tante celebrated such things? Who but she would draw symbols on the floor with flour and say blessings before adding the well-worn molar to the little clay pot that held Beatrice's other baby teeth, and nail clippings, and strands of hair taken from the comb? The pot sat on the mantel beside Tante's candles, the oiled stones in white saucers, twig crosses, a goat's horn, and bundles of dried herbs and flowers.

"You are twelve, and the moon could call to you at anytime. You best tell me as soon as it does. We'll have much to talk about."

Her meddling never failed to irritate Beatrice. Right away she had determined she'd tell Tante Perte or Tante Las first. She could decide on her own who she'd talk to. But Tante was vigilant beyond reason and knew her too well. She'd quickly taken Beatrice's face in her hands and peered into her eyes for a long, unsettling time. Tante's eyes were like black holes in a tree trunk. You couldn't be sure what hid inside them. As always, Beatrice was the first to blink and look away.

That day had been many months ago, and every week since then Tante had asked the same question until Beatrice grew weary of it, and so cross she wouldn't answer anymore. Tante called her a "late bloomer." Her thirteenth birthday was not far off, —maybe half a year—and the closer it got, the closer Tante seemed to be watching. Sometimes Beatrice woke at night and felt Tante's eyes on her, patient as an owl sitting quiet in its tree waiting for some small movement on the ground to pounce upon. So, like the mouse that knows of the owl's watching, Beatrice had learned to hide herself, and to be wary of the owl's hunger.

For all her life, she and Tante Abeille had spent most of their days together in the garden at the side of the grande maison. The garden was large and lush, and Tante talked endlessly of the flowers and creatures there, in the way she might have talked about her own children if she'd had any—as if the garden whispered secrets only she could hear.

In the past, the maison had interested Beatrice only a bit more than her own toenails did. Grand it was, but like the river, it was a part of the land-scape, always there and so she could ignore it. At least the river sometimes spilled its banks and caused a fuss. The maison cast shadows on the garden as the sun moved from morning to night, and it rotted or leaked, but it did little else.

Their master dwelled within it like an old hermit in a cave. Why the richest man in all Louisián lived alone did not concern her. She didn't wonder why he'd never hosted a fête before Lent, or a Noël ball. Having never been anywhere else, she knew of no other way he might live or behave. Aside from the celebration in the quarter following the cane harvest when casks of yeasty cane wine were brought out, she'd not been to a fête.

Slaves brought in from outside told tales of fancy women in feather masks and bright silk dresses that whispered when they danced, and of the jewels that glinted in their hair and at their throats. Of gentlemen in frock coats who slipped coins to the servants in exchange for a masked lady's name. And they described great feasts laid out on long tables, and gold-lipped goblets of fine wine, which kept everyone merry.

Beatrice couldn't imagine such liveliness inside Michie Reynard's house, but she wished to see such sights at least once in her life.

She'd seen Michie at the library window a few times, his face half hidden behind a curtain, pale as a haunt. Usually he didn't realize she'd seen him, but he had, one morning just that week. He'd quickly let the drape fall back over the panes of wavy glass, darkening them from behind. Like tall mirrors, they reflected every little thing that lay before them, but exactly backward. They were the only part of the house that Beatrice took notice of, being the only part that ever changed or hinted at life. Within them clouds and birds moved across the sky, trees swayed, the sun glimmered, seasons changed. And so did she.

Squinting at the glass just so, she thought, Looks like the garden has folded out and pushed right through the walls into Michie Reynard's house. Stones and withered petals carpeted his floors, the walls hung with blossoms and vines, and the ceiling-sky looked blue as the shell of a heron's egg. There she stood in the middle of it all, squinting back at herself from inside the windows of the house as if she belonged in it, and might even take a seat on the edge of a cushiony hedge with a teacup in her hand.

Such an idea tickled her, and seemed more right than ridiculous. Secretly she thought she'd like serving the house and Michie. Garden work was not much better than fieldwork, and being with Tante Abeille every moment had begun to feel smothery, like a dress grown too tight for comfort.

She whispered her secret wish to her reflection, then gazed past it and focused on the images that were farther away, some distance behind her. Tante pulled a malachite-colored beetle from a rosebud and flicked it over the hedge; and behind Tante, Beatrice saw a butterfly land on a hibiscus flower. It was a trick she'd discovered a year ago, not long after she'd first noticed Michie spying. Ever since then she'd practiced it: moving her sight in and out, always starting with herself and then searching deeper inside the glass. By slightly changing the way her eyes focused, she could see in two directions at the same time—forward and backward.

She'd not shared the trick with Tante, who would scold her for staring at Michie's windows so long and forbid her from doing it again. Turning away from the reflections, Beatrice said, "It must be gloomful in Michie's house. Seems like he'd look out and enjoy this garden, or walk in it."

Tante Abeille shrugged her shoulders. "I've told you before, Mamzelle Rosabel's garden doesn't bring him joy, only memories. He hasn't set a foot in it since she died of sadness. But don't you fret over that old fox, *piti*, there's nothing out here he cares to see. He's satisfied with a roomful of dusty books and the sound of his own voice."

"If Mamzelle's garden pains him so long after she died, he must have loved her."

"Pfaaa! Maybe in his own way, same as he loves everything else he owns." Abeille plucked more beetles from the blossoms of the white rose. "Mamzelle was pretty to look at, young and quiet when she wasn't weeping—she a rosebud and him a beetle. See how a beetle loves a rosebud so much that he'll chew its heart out?" She knocked one from a bud and held the ruined flower out to Beatrice as proof.

"Then why does he let the garden stay?"

"Because he promised Mamzelle I could tend it long as I lived," Abeille answered, squatting to sit back on her bare heels. "Mamzelle asked but two things of Michie after they married: to let her go home to France for a visit, and to have a pretty garden to walk in. He said no to the first, and it made her grieve till she took ill from weeping. Wouldn't rise from her bed. So he put in the garden, but it was too late. How could he refuse the third and last thing she asked? He couldn't. 'Twas at her deathbed that he promised to let me tend this garden. Once I'm gone the flowers will go, too, and then he'll plant his cane right up to them windows."

"I won't let Mamzelle's garden die," Beatrice said, forgetting the wish she'd made earlier. "I can tend it almost as well as you by now."

Abeille grunted and shook her head. "*Non*, much as I've shown you, it won't be enough. You can never learn enough." To prove it, she cupped the young bud of a peony in her hands. It was tightly clenched, a tiny green fist on a stem. Tante Abeille whispered into the cup of her hands, blew gently and slowly opened her fingers. As she did so the bud trembled. Then, layer by layer, the peony unfurled each of its petals until a fully blown red bloom filled Tante Abeille's open palms. She grinned. "One thing I truly know, Beatrice, is that your talents and mine are not the same. When I go, this garden will fail."

Stung that Tante thought so little of her skill in the garden, Beatrice set her jaw and frowned. She could do just as well as Tante without magiic tricks. A bee moved from blossom to blossom, and she followed it with her eyes. It lit beside her and pushed its dusty head into the throat of a honeysuckle flower. Gently she stroked the bee's velvety back just below its wings, a spot she'd always imagined would be perfect for a tiny saddle. She'd always liked them, even as a lap child. Had never been afraid of being stung. In fact, she had gathered them in her hands like bunches of warm raisins when she was smaller, shivering at their tickling feet on her skin.

The bee buzzed against her fingertip and a picture flashed behind her eyes, a burst of sharp, colored light that disappeared before she could focus on it. A bittersweet smokiness flavored the back of her tongue. She recognized it immediately. The air at harvest always tasted of burned sugar-cane, but that season was months away yet.

She closed her eyes and concentrated on the ghost of the image burned into the backs of her eyelids in the manner of a sunspot. Doing so was akin to looking at the window reflections, but more difficult, a bit like watching something on the slant, without turning directly to it. Her eye sockets throbbed with the effort of focusing, but finally she saw.

It was a dark hole cut into the earth, more long than wide, and deep enough to be a grave. Empty, but not for long. This she understood, somehow. And it seemed that if she tried very hard she could know to whom the hole belonged. All she had to do was strain further, or take a step toward it. . . .

"*Non!*" she gasped, and quickly pressed the heels of her palms into her eyes to scrub the image away. The hole wanted to swallow her, trap her, but she wouldn't let it.

Her head pounded. She felt dizzy, unbalanced. A wave of nausea pushed up from the pit of her belly and flooded her mouth with spittle. These fits had begun with the onset of spring. They grew stronger each time, insistent as newly sprouted seeds pushing toward light.

She knew well that her *maman*, Ara, had been plagued by fits. Maman had gone raving mad in the end. She had thrown herself in the river on the very day she gave birth, hadn't she? She'd wanted nothing to do with her own baby daughter.

A fisherman in a boat had rescued Maman before she drowned, but she had cursed him for his trouble. Everybody who remembered that day said Maman screamed without stopping when he brought her ashore. They recalled how her voice sounded shrill as a screech owl's, and that she'd spewed odd words none of them understood—nonsense and gibberish.

Not long after that, the poor fisherman's boat hit a stump and sank in the river. He had swum ashore, but couldn't earn a living without his boat. Bad luck had dogged him every day since—proof that Ara had been a witch. And whatever had possessed her was passed to the girl-baby she'd birthed that day. To them, Beatrice was *hibou*—screech owl—and so they made the gesture against evil if ever she looked their way.

Beatrice took her palms from her eyes and blinked. The throbbing inside her head slowed to match her heartbeat, and the picture of the grave faded to shadowy memory. She could almost believe it hadn't happened at all, if not for her lingering dizziness.

Tante Abeille grasped her arm, startling her. The old woman's grip held firm as she pulled herself up from the ground and steadied herself. She let go and said, "I'm going down to the pasture to check the hives. It's been a while since I've looked in on the bees."

"Take me with you?" Beatrice blurted, still troubled.

Abeille brushed the air with her fingers dismissively. "They'd sting you. Bees don't take kindly to strangers near their hives. It's terrible to die of bee stings. I know a man who nearly did. His tongue swelled up like a fat sausage, and he almost choked on it. He shouldn't have gone where he didn't belong and wasn't wanted. You stay away from my hives or you'll upset the bees and spoil the honey."

"You always say that, but the bees never sting

me in the garden. And besides that, you wouldn't let them sting me."

"Pfaaa! What could I do to keep them from it? You stay right here and finish pinching beetles from this rose. Do it well, and go straight to the cookhouse to help Las and Perte before it gets dark." She reached out to pat Beatrice's cheek, but Beatrice tilted her face away.

Tante Abeille did not move her hand from the place Beatrice's face had been. She let her fingers linger in the empty air before she curled them to her palm and slowly lowered her arm. "Pout if you want, but mind you don't sneak behind me. I'll know if you do."

Beatrice remained silent. She looked up only after Tante had gone. Angrily she bent and yanked at the clumps of chicken weed sprouting between the bricks that bordered the flowerbed. A wretched flowerbed, always abloom with Tante's wretched flowers. She reached in, uprooted a pink-and-white lily, and flung it over her shoulder in a satisfying spray of dirt. Two more followed the first. A hibiscus, in full bloom, was more stubborn. As she tugged at it the feeling of unease returned, the spidery sense of being watched. Perhaps the old man was peeking from behind his curtains, angry at what she was doing.

She pivoted to face the windows, thinking that this time she'd be bold enough to meet his eyes. Three boys stood just outside the garden fence with their backs to the looking-glass windows. Beatrice's heart flittered like a bird trapped inside a willow basket, but she lifted her chin and glared at the oldest of them, Kerel, who Tante had said was Bea's "milk twin." As newborns they'd shared his mother and her milk between them.

Kerel worked as the bellows boy for the plantation blacksmith. He reminded her of the red roosters that roamed about the quarter: proud, sharp-tongued, and mean. He had a curiously hairless face, without eyelashes or eyebrows. Tante said the fire from the forge kept everything singed away, even the fuzz on his arms and hands. And sure enough, his skin was spattered with small dark scars that'd come from the embers sent flying by the bellows.

He cupped his hands around his mouth and hooted like an owl. The two younger boys followed his example. *"Hibou!"* one of them jeered, while the other began hooting. Kerel had something dark in his hand, a stone or a brown egg. He cocked back and threw it as he yelled, "I brought your dinner, *hibou!*"

A dead water rat sailed past Beatrice's ear and landed beside her in the flowers. The second one hit the side of her head and knocked her head scarf askew. Before she could scramble to her feet, all three boys touched fingers and thumbs together and pushed their hands out in the gesture against evil, and then ducked around the corner of the maison.

With all her heart she hated them! Tante would tell her to ignore their foolishness, but how could she? If only she knew the curses Maman had used on the boatman. More than anything, she wanted to fix those rotten boys. Kerel first and most, and then everyone who called her *hibou*, or made that sign in her direction.

Shaking with anger, she straightened her *tignon*, pushing beneath it the strands of hair that had escaped. One rat lay on the brick path, stiff with death, its fur still damp where one of the mouser cats had gnawed it. Beatrice searched for the other rat among the flowers, knowing it would stink if she left it there. It had landed in the raw place where she'd torn out a lily. On a flower stem near the rat, the shed skin of a cicada clung like a blown seedpod.

She and Tante dug them up sometimes, these fat grubs that lived underground. And she imagined them in their dark tunnels, chewing roots, complacent. Until a night came when the creatures felt a sudden and powerful call, one that drove them toward the surface, sent them climbing cane stalks and tree trunks and fence posts to shrug off their old skins.

"If they've never seen moonlight, how do they know it's there?" she asked Tante Abeille.

"How do they even know to look for it?"

"A faith stronger than ours, *piti*. They never doubt themselves, as we do."

"You sound like the père when he talks about the church's saints."

Tante had cackled like a hen pleased to have laid an egg. "The père has his church and his saints, and I have mine."

The rise-and-fall throb of the cicadas' chorus in the trees and cane fields reminded Beatrice of the shivery noise made by Tante Abeille's *asson*—a rattle she kept as a sacred thing. It was made of simple materials: a dried calabash gourd emptied of seeds, its outside netted over with strands of colored beads, and inside, the small round bones of a snake's back to make the noise. An *asson* put in righteous hands could call the *loa*.

Beatrice slid the tip of her smallest finger inside the split where the new cicada had escaped its skin, as if her own flesh were the insect trying to reclaim a lost life.

CHAPTER FOUR

Needle

EATRICE hurried along the whistler's path that led from the back of the maison to the cookhouse. She'd not finished the weeding, or plucked beetles from the rose as Tante Abeille had asked. Her anger at Kerel had cooled, but it had left her feeling bruised-hearted and anxious to be away from the garden.

As she drew nearer to the cookhouse, she heard Tante Perte whistling as clear as a redbird. Anyone who carried Michie's food to the table had to whistle, because a busy mouth couldn't steal a taste from the dishes. Tante Perte hadn't delivered a tray in many years, not since she became cook, but she still whistled out of habit while she worked.

The smell of gumbo and simmering rice met Beatrice at the door, as did the heat from the hearth fire. Tante Las, who was so thin she never felt warm, sat near the firebox mending the hem of a bedsheet while Tante Perte stirred a steaming pot. Without turning away from it she said, "There's our Bea come back to the hive, Las." Her voice was as warm and comforting as the smell of the food, and Las's smile was equally welcoming.

Beatrice wrapped her arms around Perte's broad, damp shoulders, grateful to be loved. "How do you know it's me and not one of the babies come to beg a lump of sugar?"

"I still see a bit at the edges, I'm not all blind. And, other than Abeille, you're the only one fills up a room with the smell of garden dirt and rose petals." Tante Perte passed Beatrice a steaming bowl of gumbo, and Beatrice placed it on a silver service tray already set with dinner dishes and a basket of bread. She covered the bowl with a saucer and then draped a cloth over everything.

Tante Las glanced up from her mending. "A few more stitches, and I'll take that inside. The old man can wait another minute." She bent so that her face was close to the cloth. Gnarled fingers pushed the needle in and out, making stitches as neat and small and straight as the tracks of an ant. Finally she pulled the thread up and snapped it between her teeth. Just as soon as she did, the silver needle fell from her grasp to the floor.

She gave a little cry, and held up her crooked fingers in disgust. "These old claws just don't work anymore the way I want or need of them. Now they've let go my last needle." She struck them against her legs. "*Zut!* I dread asking Michie to order new. Hasn't been long enough since I asked for the last." She peered down at the floor so that the creases in her face deepened and made her look very old and weary.

"I can take the tray inside," Beatrice offered. "Then you won't have to ask."

Tante Las shook her head. "Be it today or tomorrow, I got no choice but ask him. And Abeille would wring my neck if I sent you to Michie. I'd be more feared of that."

"She's with her hives, and she told me to help you," Beatrice said, her voice sharp, defiant.

"You don't whistle," Tante Perte reminded her. "And Las is the one Michie'd be expecting. He's peculiar about such things—worries someone will poison him, or put glass in his food, or some other foolishness. Stay here and use your good eyes to find Las's needle. That would be a better help."

Beatrice remembered the vision that had come in the garden, and doubted the goodness of her eyes, hexed like Maman's. Still, she did have a talent for finding, a thing different from but akin to seeing. In the same way she'd learned to shift her sight back and forth to see deeper reflections in the windows, she'd learned to seek what was hidden or lost: buttons, coins, and whatnot. It was her own secret, and she trusted it in a way that she didn't trust visions.

Kneeling on the floor, she said, "Wait before you ask Michie for a new one, Tante Las. I'll have your needle by the time you come back."

With eyes closed, she settled her mind and concentrated on seeing the sliver of silver, and then on seeing it in Tante Las's fingers just before it slipped. She saw Tante snap the thread between her teeth, and then slowly, as if through oil and not air, the needle fell. She made it large in her mind and supposed the path it had taken, beginning with its landing place beside Tante Las's right foot. From there her thoughts followed as it tumbled and bounced tip to end, end to tip, then rolled until it reached a crack between two bricks at the edge of the hearth.

She opened her eyes, and without speaking, crawled to the hearth and ran her hands over the bricks beside the basket of mending. She stopped where she thought she must and whispered, "Here, I think." From the broom leaning against the wall she broke a straw and asked Tante Perte to dip it in honey. When that was done she poked the sticky lure into the narrow crack and traced its length. Soon she lifted the needle like a minnow caught on a line. "I have it!" she said, surprised and pleased.

"Small miracles are still miracles!" Tante Perte crowed, clapping her hands together. "Las will be relieved, sure enough."

Miracle or magiic or luck, Beatrice didn't know. She only knew that the look of relief on the old woman's face when she returned to the cookhouse dulled the hurt Kerel had given her. It was with lighter hearts that she and her tantes sat down to share what was left of the gumbo, spooning it into their mouths directly from the cookpot.

Tante Perte and Tante Las's love was easier than Tante Abeille's, Beatrice thought. They rarely

scolded, and made few demands. They spoke of
Maman with kindness, while Tante Abeille spoke
of her, if at all, with bitter disappointment. Reason
again not to talk about the visions in the garden.
Who wanted to be equally as disappointing as
Maman?

Tante Perte and Tante Las put their spoons
down before the pot was emptied, letting Beatrice
have a larger portion. Tante Las pinched a bit of
snuff from her tin and returned to her chair and
her mending by the hearth, and Tante Perte joined
her.

When she'd finished eating, and had scoured
the dishes and cookery, and swept the floor,
Beatrice left them watching the last embers of the
hearth fire burn down.

After the pent-in heat of the cookhouse, the
night air seemed cooler than it was, and sweet with
the smell of garden flowers: magnolia and honeysuckle and rose. She remembered the rats still lying
in the garden. By morning they'd be swollen like

furred cucumbers and swarming with blowflies that would bite and pester her and Tante Abeille all day long. The thought sent a fresh rush of anger through her. She'd have to go back and fetch the reeking carcasses Kerel had thrown at her.

Though it was evenfall, and the bricks of the path that led to the garden were buckled and uneven in places, she knew them well enough not to trip. The flattened, grayish light threw deep shadows at the feet of the maison so that it looked as though it stood at the edge of a dark pond. All the windows were dark but those of the library.

Golden lamplight seeped along the edges of the heavy curtains as Beatrice opened the gate a crack and entered the garden. The soft hum of bees hovering among flowers had been replaced by the shrill voices of crickets hidden in the mulch. She moved slowly and carefully along the path so as not to step on one of the rats by accident. She'd gone half the way when she heard the gate hinges squeal and the latch click. Turning, she expected to see

Tante Abeille, but the silhouette coming toward her had more bulk and moved too slowly to be Tante. The blacksmith walked with a similar limp, but she knew it wasn't him—it was Michie Reynard who walked toward her on the shadowy path.

An ebony cane with a carved ivory knob bore his weight. He looked mushroom pale and held a cloth to his nose with his free hand, as though breathing the air outside offended him. He stopped short when he saw her.

"It's late," he called out, clearly annoyed. "Why are you here?"

Beatrice's heart turned to a lump of clay and traveled up to her throat. She'd worked in the shadow of his house nearly every day, but he'd never spoken directly to her that she could remember. Lost for words with which to answer him, she dropped her gaze to the ground. Tante Abeille had taught her what she should do: look at your feet, speak only to answer a question, be polite, and always keep a safe distance.

He drew closer, and she stepped backward. His hand atop the carved fox-head knob held her gaze, for his knuckles were as white as the polished bone. "I've asked you a question, my girl!" he barked.

Beatrice took a deep breath, letting her words ride forth in a rush. "Pardon, Michie, I didn't think to find anyone . . ."

He broke in with an entirely different question before she finished with the first. "Why not?"

The question caught her off guard entirely. She couldn't stop from looking up to search his face for some clue to the correct answer. What light there was revealed heavy lids and bristling gray brows that shaded his eyes; and a thick mustache that appeared to sprout from inside his nose hid his upper lip. But the loose skin of his jowls was clean-shaven, and beneath it his jaw muscles twitched with impatience.

"Tante Abeille says you never come here," she blurted.

"I prefer to come here when she's gone. What else does she say?"

Terrified, Beatrice whispered, "You like to look at the pages of books more than walk in the garden."

"Because books are not full of bees and quarrelsome crones," he interrupted, and took another step toward her.

This time Beatrice was forced to hold her ground; another step or two back would put her on top of the rat. She shook her head and clasped her hands together, half in prayer and half to hide their trembling.

Reynard harrumphed and looked about the garden with disdain. He jabbed his cane at the large white rosebush as if skewering someone with a sword. A handful of startled beetles took flight, spinning recklessly into the darkness with the clicking sound of fingernails drawn over a washboard. One landed on his lapel and crawled upward, no doubt looking for a proper launching place. He grimaced and flicked it away quickly.

Tante said he was always wary of creatures that might sting.

Worried that he was pointing out her and Tante Abeille's failings at tending the garden, Beatrice rushed forward flapping her hands at the rose. She cried, "*Mon chagren!* Tante told me to pluck the beetles off today, and I didn't."

"Don't you do what you are told?"

"Nearly always I do. . . ."

"Don't you like your work?"

"Not always." Beatrice clamped her hand over her mouth, horrified that she was flustered enough to say such a thing.

But he laughed, a soft rumbling inside his throat. "You're honest. Are you not afraid of me?"

She looked at him from beneath her lashes and whispered, *"Oui."*

He smiled and considered her for a moment. "Of course you are, Abeille would have made you afraid. But you mustn't be. I am in need of someone young to serve my table, and dust and sweep and answer when I call. Today I realized Las has grown too old and slow."

Beatrice's mouth dropped open. To become a servant of the maison would mean she would never be sent to the cane fields or the sugarhouse or to any other hard labor. And it also would mean being under Michie's constant watch, always at his beckoning, with new rules, and more expected. Everyone in the quarter had a day of rest except those who served the maison. Still, it was a prize, and it would mean time away from Tante Abeille's constant eye—a wish come true.

"What would happen to Tante Las?" Beatrice wondered aloud.

"She's still a good laundress. She can sit by the hearth and mend socks, and help Perte with the kitchen."

Tante Las wouldn't be sent away. Beatrice was relieved. "But I can't whistle. Not a note."

Reynard held her in his gaze for a long while, already taking measure of her failures she was sure—

but then he laughed. It wasn't a happy sound, something akin to wheezy coughing. He dabbed his handkerchief to his mouth, then mopped his brow and said, "Whistling is a vulgar habit for a pretty young lady, I think. Ladies may hum."

Beatrice stood still as a garden statue as he tottered away. In a few moments his shadow moved inside the lit room. Outside, a wizzygig of lacewings and katydids and brown moths hurled themselves at the glass like thrown pebbles.

All her life she'd been called Honey Bea, niece, Ara's girl, garden girl, witch, *hibou, sang mêlé*, and worse—but never a pretty young lady. She said it aloud and felt herself stand a little straighter, her chin lift, her heart beat faster. He'd planted something in her too small to think of or put into words, like the tiny gray seed of a poppy.

CHAPTER FIVE

Mawu

EATRICE retrieved the dead rats from the garden. Rather than put the rats on the trash heap, she carried them through the dark to the smith's shop. It was the size of the cookhouse, but enclosed on just three sides by walls of brick and timber. An open chimney with a raised hearth jutted from the longest wall at the back. Anvils of different sizes crowded the hearth's edge, and a selection of hammers and tongs lay about. Some fire still glowed in the heart of the firebox, enough that Beatrice could make out the bellows hanging from a hook to the right of the chimney, and with it a pair of long, leather work gloves. She reasoned that they belonged to Kerel, to keep the fire from cooking his hands while he worked.

Carefully she opened one and stuffed the first rat deep inside it. She filled the second glove with the second rat and rubbed her hands on her skirt. The clearest image of Kerel pulling on his left glove struck her: his startled face, his hand jerking away from the damp fur, nose wrinkling at the stench, mouth letting go a string of curses. Satisfaction glowed inside her, warm as the embers in the firebox, as she crept back out to the lane.

The moon had risen fully above the trees by the time she set foot on her own cabin porch. Tante Abeille was waiting for her. Her eyes were hard, black stones set in a face of parched river mud. "You are late," she said, her voice low and accusing.

Beatrice had already worked out what should be told and what should not. She needn't tell about Kerel—she'd taken care of that herself—but her meeting with Michie couldn't be kept a secret, and so she recounted it. "He called me 'a pretty young lady,' Tante," she said, surprised at how happy it made her to repeat the words aloud.

Tante Abeille listened quietly, her mouth a tense, grim line. She remained quiet for so long that Beatrice grew uncomfortable. Finally Tante Abeille took up a washbasin and put her face inside it, saying, "Cotch our words, like a net cotch fish. Let none escape to come back and bite us."

With one quick motion she turned the basin over and put it on the cabin floor. She glared at Beatrice, and her voice trembled with anger when she spoke. "Reynard speaks with a forked tongue. What he says is always for his own good and no one else's. He wants something."

"I have nothing he'd want."

"Only a child would think that."

Beatrice blushed at what Tante suggested, but the contempt she heard in the old woman's voice fueled an answering spite in her own. "I am not a child anymore; I can judge what he wants from me."

"Phfft! You have much to learn if you think he wants nothing."

"You are the one who always wants; who is always looking for something from me."

Tante Abeille's open palm struck the side of her face. "What I want is to help you claim what he doesn't already own. . . ."

Beatrice did not wait to hear any more. With her cheek aflame and her ear ringing, she rushed from the cabin. Her feet ran where they wanted—toward the cookhouse. But the window of the little room at the back where Tante Perte and Tante Las slept was shuttered and dark.

She knew their day started before dawn and ended after dark. She hesitated to wake them. They'd more than earned the short rest that sleep brought to them. Looking beyond the cookhouse, she saw that light still spilled from the library windows. She crept toward them, the mossy path beneath her feet cold and comforting as she entered the garden.

Without thought she crawled into the space beneath the arching canes of the white rose. There she curled up on the thick litter of leaves and fragrant old petals, nearly choking on the anger that clotted in her throat. Tears slid from the corners of her eyes and filled her ears, spilling over to dampen the soil behind her neck.

As a little girl, she'd taken refuge in the rose arbor when Tante scolded her, or the other girls teased her, but she'd never lain beneath it at night with the moon and stars peeking between the branches. *Mawu* was what Tante called the moon. She said it had a woman's spirit. Far across a wide salt sea, in Afrik—where their ancestors had once owned themselves—women built altars for Mawu long ago, fed her from their tables, and even spoke to her. When the moon was fullest, they danced a circle in gratitude for rain, or a good harvest, or with hopes that someone might be healed or favored. And Mawu did bless those who honored her with special gifts linked to earth and water and air.

Beatrice stared through the leaves at the waning moon. Sharp-tipped and silvered as the rose's thorns, it seemed to grow and pull her toward it, the distance closing in so that she could almost see Mawu's face peering at her from the shadowed side.

Frightened, she closed her eyes tight and turned to hide her face from the moonlight. All around, the rose leaves worried and whispered in her ears with every breeze that blew—murmuring with the voices of spirits whose breath smelled of earthworms and wet stone and leaf mold.

It seemed that she had only just fallen asleep when the first cock crowed his challenge to the rising sun. Other cocks joined in from wherever they'd roosted during the night. Beatrice lay still, recollecting where she'd bedded, and why, before opening her eyes. Rose canes arched over her head in a green tangle. Here and there hazy light pierced the canopy in narrow beams that looked like the blades of sabers. One shone on her hand and warmed it. When she moved to rub her eyes, the leaf duff beneath her hand shifted so that the stream of light met uncovered ground. A metallic wink caught her eye. Likely a shard of moonstone, she thought, and scratched the dirt aside to see it. She found instead a silver oval the size of a shelled walnut—the top half of a broken locket.

Beatrice crawled outside the bower. Using her fingernail, she scraped away the embedded dirt, then moistened a corner of her skirt with spittle and wiped the locket clean. A raised relief of vines and flowers covered the front. The smooth inner face was etched with a small, looping script. Beatrice turned it round in her palm, wondering what the symbols meant. No one she knew could decipher writing except Michie and the overseer's wife, but she'd never dare ask either of them.

They'd only take the locket from her, for she felt it might have once belonged to Mamzelle Rosabel.

Now the silver oval lay warm and lovely in Beatrice's hand, the prettiest thing she'd ever held, and she intended to keep it. She tucked it in her pocket, straightened her *tignon,* and dusted her hands on her skirt. Already there were honeybees at work in the garden. Had Tante Abeille got worried and gone looking for her during the night? She would have been quiet about it, not wanting anyone to think Beatrice had run off, not wanting to draw attention. They all knew the overseer had his spies in the quarter; those who hoped to gain a favor or take revenge by telling secrets, or even lies.

Beatrice was in the kitchen before Tante Perte or Las awoke, and had the fire stoked and bread rising by the time they tottered in, still stiff-limbed from sleep. She gave them mugs of steaming chicory to sip before she told them that Michie Reynard had asked her to leave the garden to serve him.

The warmth in the kitchen seemed to evaporate.

"Does Abeille know?" Tante Perte asked.

"*Oui*," Beatrice answered, "but what she thinks doesn't matter. Michie decides." They were quiet. She spoke the truth.

When the breakfast tray was ready, Beatrice took a deep breath and closed her fingers around its handles. It weighed more than she'd thought. Her arms trembled with the effort of lifting. The dishes rattled like the sound of chattering teeth as she carried the tray along the whistler's path and up the back steps. She hummed because that's what Michie had asked, and it comforted her, too. The song was an old lullaby that sometimes popped into her head when she least expected it, but she didn't know the words, if there were any.

When she reached the library, the door was closed. She banged against it with her elbow, trying not to spill.

"Come in," Reynard called from the other side.

Beatrice stared at the door handle, dumbfounded. How to open it without letting go of the tray and dropping everything? How did Tante Las do it? She balanced it on one raised knee and then the other, but could not safely let go.

"The latch . . ." she called out, defeated.

A chair scraped against the wooden floor, followed by labored footsteps. The door swung open and Michie stood before her as he had in the garden, but more at ease in this room full of neatly shelved books.

She set the tray down on a table before the hearth, careful not to spill, then dipped her head in a half-curtsy and moved to take her station out in the hall, as Tante Las had instructed her. But Reynard closed the door and gestured toward a small wooden step stool used to reach the books on the highest shelves.

She hesitated, remembering Tante Abeille's warning about his motives. Unable to disobey, she sank down onto the stool, perching at the front edge and tucking her legs and bare feet beneath her skirt. She ignored the feel of his eyes on her by studying the room intently. A part of her had expected to find it filled up with the garden, just as she pictured it from the outside. She couldn't have imagined this, however, because she'd never seen such splendor.

There was painted wood trim carved to resemble gapped teeth, and gleaming walls paneled with another wood that had been sliced and oiled to reveal a natural flame pattern in its grain. Her feet pushed into the deep nap of a fine wool carpet that covered the floor, and she thought it not so different from the moss that grew on the brick path. Near one window, a wide desk rested upon feet that looked like the talons of a great owl or hawk clutching a ball. And a reading chair covered in tufted red leather sat beside the wide hearth near the second window—the one from which she'd seen him spying on her.

As usual the drapes were closed, and the room felt uncomfortably warm and humid and close. A "dead house" was what Tante Perte would call it. A house that didn't breathe and had too little life inside it would soon rot away. Beatrice resisted the urge to throw open the sash and let a sweet breeze from the garden clean out the stale smell and move the air.

She studied the rows of colored leather books that lined the wall shelves, their spines marked with what looked like chicken tracks and curling snail trails, and wondered why anyone needed so many. Tante Abeille said he kept secrets pressed between the pages of books the way Mamzelle Rosabel had once pressed flowers. "He think he can keep the truth locked up tight till it fade and turn to dust. *Mais oui*, he think he can master even that, but no one can forever. Not him, nor me." What that meant, Beatrice couldn't guess and didn't try. Tante trusted nothing about Michie.

I am old enough to decide for myself, Beatrice told herself. She touched the cheek Tante had slapped. Still sore.

Her eyes settled on a book spine that bore a single mark, the only letter she knew. The golden *R* with chest thrown out and one foot stepping forward was printed or burned into many of the things Michie owned: the shipping barrels that held sugar and molasses and rice at the end of harvest time, and the hide of every work animal; and there was a large *R* curled in the center of the fancy iron gate that closed off the carriage lane of the maison from the River Road—a gate forged by the blacksmith, Monsieur Gú, who had the letter branded on his forehead.

Michie ate quietly, sipping his coffee without taking his eyes from her. Finally he wiped his mustache with a napkin and smiled, though there was little warmth in it. He held a basket of sugared beignets out toward her. "Take one," he said. "Your grandmère loved them."

Surprised, Bea did as he asked. She held the warm bread in her palm without eating it.

"Does Abeille ever speak to you of her sister, Derora?"

"Only to say they were twins, that Grandmère worked in this house, and she died after she gave birth to my mother."

Reynard pursed his lips for a moment. He seemed perplexed. "That's all she's said in all your years? Nothing else?"

"Not much more, Michie, nothing important," Bea answered, cautious now. An unseen and dangerous current ran beneath his words, one that could pull her feet from beneath her if she wasn't careful.

He rose and walked to the shelves behind his desk and pulled a book from it—the one with the narrow black spine and gold *R*. He flipped through the pages, stopped, ran his finger down one side of it. "Here you are—Beatrice, born to Ara, and she born to Derora . . ."

He considered the page more closely. "Your grandmère's name should be on this line beside Abeille's, but the ink is quite faded now; her name is nearly lost." Wrinkling his brow, he moved his face closer to the paper and squinted. "My eyesight fails me. So many things fail me of late."

He rubbed his eyes with his thumbs and

gestured toward the opposite wall at a portrait of a young woman wearing a gown as pale as buttermilk. She held her hands clasped together at her narrow waist, the stem of a single white rose folded in her fingers. Her eyes were the blue of open sky, but melancholy and touched with some gray—a sky before rain. She gazed at something just outside the picture's frame with such longing that Beatrice wished to help her find it.

"That is my wife, Rosabel," he said, pulling Beatrice's thoughts away from the painting. "A failure. She never bore a child. Had we been blessed in that way, I might now have grandchildren. Instead, I am left alone in my age."

He stopped speaking and turned away from the portrait. The hardness crept back over his face and into his eyes, as if he suddenly realized Beatrice was still in the room.

He jabbed his finger at the page open before him. "Abeille stole Derora's body from the casket I had brought from N'Orléans. Polished wood with a lining of white silk. No slave ever lay in something so fine, but Abeille took Derora from it during the night and buried her in a raw hole like an onion bulb, like a dead cat.

"At the very least I wanted the père to bless her grave but Abeille refused to take us to it. She hated Derora. Always jealous."

"Jealous of her sister?"

Reynard raised his brows in surprise. "Of course! Because I sent Abeille away to the quarter when Rosabel died, but kept Derora. For a while I was sure it wasn't childbirth that had killed Derora, but Abeille. There were rumors. . . ."

Rainwater washed through Beatrice's veins. Why had she never heard these things? Not even from Tante Perte or Tante Las. She stood clumsily and pushed her mouth into an empty, troubled smile. "Should I take your tray, Michie?"

"*Oui*, I am tired." He bent and frowned deeply at the page before him. Hunched as he was over his desk, he looked frail and old. His scalp shone baby pink through the thin wisps of white hair he'd combed over the top of his head, and his hand tremored as he dipped his pen nib in an inkpot and scratched it across the paper to fill in Derora's lost name.

He looked up once more, but this time Beatrice could not cast her eyes away from his. Rather than the anger she expected, his eyes looked sad and rheumy with the glaze of age. Melancholy as the woman's in the painting, and with the same longing, they searched her own. A brief, wan smile touched his lips before he lowered his gaze back to the papers on his desk.

Through the glass behind Reynard's bent head Beatrice caught sight of the garden. The blossoms of the white rose nodded gently, bathed by the light of early morning. "Mamzelle's rose," Abeille called it, and it was the rose the slender painted hands of Rosabel held. Beatrice realized then that the portrait's sad blue eyes did indeed gaze beyond the frame; at the rose named for her, at the garden, and at all that might be beyond it.

CHAPTER SIX

Reynard

REYNARD waited for several minutes after the girl had gone before he looked up from the ledger on his desk. He took a deep breath, hoping her scent still lingered in the room. Though she was younger than her grandmère had been when he first saw her, Beatrice was very like Derora: lovely to behold, fittingly humble, but with a quiet dignity and sweet charm that surprised.

He placed his pen on a small tray and rubbed

the clean-shaven folds of his neck with a shaking hand that showed truly what he preferred to hide: he'd grown old, and for all the years that had passed, Derora still had hold of him. She had not aged in his memory beyond the young woman he'd first seen at work in a cane field shortly after his marriage to Rosabel.

He hadn't realized Derora and Abeille were sisters, much less twins. They'd been purchased in a lot with twenty others in N'Orléans, and if the overseer knew the two were sisters, he hadn't bothered to tell Reynard. To most anyone's eye, the two sisters weren't a match—Abeille was a clot of dirt with a crow's voice, while Derora was a sunny brook with a voice sweet and silvery as a thrush's.

There in his cane field, Derora dipped so gracefully as she pushed her allotment of seed cane into the ridge of a long row, just as a lady might curtsy to a gentleman at a ball. Soil darkened her dress hem and hands, sweat moistened her face; but she enchanted him nonetheless with her lovely slanted eyes and dark skin the color of burned caramel. He admired her from atop his horse for a long while, and realized he needed to see such beauty every day.

Rosabel's beauty didn't move him. She was pretty in her way, porcelain fragile and dainty. But whatever small flame might have burned in him for her had been doused by her tedious weeping and whining. His mother, Madame Rillieux, had proposed the marriage. Rosabel was the youngest daughter of a family she socialized with in Paris. Rosabel's family had a good name but little money. He had money and required a wife of *qualité*, and so like all else in his life, the marriage was a business arrangement. Unfortunately her noble blood proved to be thin as donkey's milk and her heart was as delicate as a primrose petal.

Derora was his wife's opposite in every way: mahogany where the other was ivory, ripe fruit where the other was stalk, wool rather than flax, cider instead of milk. He brought her in from the field the day he laid eyes on her and put her to work in the maison as a housemaid.

His mother would have sensed the danger immediately had she been there. She'd have snapped her fan at the end of his nose and waved it like a baton while she scolded him. "You are a Rillieux! Your grandpère was pure French, a person of *qualité*, a nobleman. If you must have a mistress then you will find a Creole girl in Orléans to consort with rather than a common field hand."

Fortunately Madame Rillieux had returned to France following Reynard's wedding to Rosabel, without plans to return. She'd found him a suitable wife to take her place in the grande maison and she preferred a life in Paris to her life on a cane farm. So long as he kept her bank account full, she left him alone.

Derora learned her tasks quickly. When he spoke to her she responded carefully, as all his servants did, nothing more. Nothing to lure him as he wished she would. Her modesty made her lovelier, and he soon felt his heart leave him for Derora as it never had for Rosabel. He found himself craving the sight and sound of her, felt starved if an hour went by without her. He had never been so beguiled by any woman. He thought himself above such foolishness, and here his heart trotted after this one like a stupid lap dog.

He drank brandy to cure himself, with no success. Derora cast a slow, potent spell with no more than her warm scent in a room, the sound of her skirts moving about her legs, and her long-toed feet peeking out, dark as the floorboards. Her strong, work-callused hands smoothing his bedsheets in the morning, and the thumb-sized hollow between neck and breastbone seen as she bent forward, made his heart ache. Made him grind his teeth when he slept, dreaming always of her.

As her master, he could have done with her whatever he wanted without permission. But he didn't want her to fear him, or to dread being in his company. Equally he didn't want Rosabel to send

word of his actions to Madame in Paris. *Non!*
Madame couldn't hear of it, or she'd return home
and take matters into her own hands.

He had the elaborate garden put in, hoping
Rosabel would spend all her time there so he could
pursue Derora more openly. He knew he must
court her, rather than force himself on her. Try as
he might, she deflected every advance, refused every
gift, and finally asked to return to the fields.

He'd been desperate then; desperate enough to
consider the sort of violence he'd sworn he'd not
use against her; desperate enough to seek the devil's
help. He'd called Rosabel's maid, Abeille, to him
and asked if she knew of a spell-worker in the
quarter, someone who could work a love charm.

"Who needs this charm?" she asked. "Man or
woman?"

"A man who'd like a lady to fall in love with
him."

"This man is you?"

Her directness and impertinence surprised

him, threw him off his guard. Though he didn't answer yes or no, he saw that Abeille had already guessed the truth. Before he could sputter out an indignant denial, she began nodding her head. "*Oui*, this is a fine idea! Love can banish tears as easily as it can bring them. If Mamzelle were to fall in love, she might be cured of this terrible melancholy. And who better to fall in love with than her own husband, eh?"

How could he have disagreed with her? "The perfect remedy," he said. "Do you know where I can come by such a charm?"

She assured him that she did, and brought it to him the very next day. He didn't question her other than ask how long he must wait for results.

"It is potent," she answered simply.

He'd been pleasantly surprised at how rapidly the spell worked. For a glorious time it had been like Eden inside the walls of his house, with nothing in the world but Derora and him.

Abeille quickly realized his trickery, but her

rage didn't concern him. Rosabel fell ill and took to her bed soon after Derora fell in love with him, but his wife's sudden death had been a relief more than a sadness. He was able to court Derora without guilt. He banished Abeille from the maison for good, though her presence lingered.

Life before Derora became a wisp of memory —less than a dream.

But she vanished like a dream, too. Gone without so much as a grave to visit—Abeille had stolen even that from him. He opened a drawer and took from it all that he had left of Derora: her white *tignon*, left behind on the casket's silk pillow.

He was old and weak-eyed now; Derora's likeness hadn't been captured on a canvas, but he pictured her face so clearly. It flickered in his mind like a pearl of light in a dark, wintry place of longest nights—immeasurably long and lonely to consider. He wanted springtime light again, steady and warming, to push the crowding shadows back and melt the creeping frost that chilled his bones.

Beatrice can be that light, he told himself with certainty, and hope.

He'd watched her grow up like a flower in the garden, her care the only reason he let Abeille stay. Now he dared to wonder if the girl wasn't Derora come back to him. Was Beatrice a seer, too? Could she cure him of the terrible *mal* that gnawed his core like a grub inside a pecan? Soon he'd be so hollow even the hungry grub would abandon him. Leave him empty. Leave him alone.

Nothing pleased him anymore, not his cane fields, or the money cane brought him, or the things money bought. Not strong wine, or the savor of food, or a tuneful song, or story well told. He kept a lamp burning beside his bed all night, for he had nothing but ugly nightmares when he slept. He saw himself locked inside a tiny cell, and his own slaves peered at him through the little window in the door. He wanted food, and they threw in billets of dry cane. He asked for water, and they spat on the floor. He demanded to be let out, and they laughed at him. He begged for a candle when night came, but no one listened.

Mais oui, just one night's sleep with a peaceful mind would please him more than anything. He might trade all his holdings in exchange for a day and a night of peace, if it could be promised.

Before he put Derora's *tignon* away he held it to his nose for a moment. The scent of her hair lingered in the scrap of cloth—river water and oleander. He put the *tignon* aside and closed the ledger before him, and then rose from his desk chair with a grunt and a wince. As he returned the book to its slot on the shelf, his arm trembled with the weight of it.

Beatrice stepped lightly as she toted the tray from the maison back to the cookhouse. In the hallway she'd stuffed the entire beignet Michie had given her into her mouth. Swallowing the last of it, she licked sugar crystals from her lips.

Tante Abeille had made her frightened of

Michie, all because she carried an old grudge. She pointed fingers and accused him of secrets when she had many of her own, it seemed. What else had she not told Beatrice? What was she hiding?

The heavy scent of the rose arbor sweetened the morning air, and the cicadas had just begun to rattle the cane with their noise. As Beatrice passed the garden, she slowed and listened for the sounds of Tante Abeille at her work. The *thwack* of spade into dirt told her that the old woman was turning soil in one of the beds, readying it for new plantings.

Ordinarily she would have called out a greeting to Tante Abeille, but this time she didn't. And she decided she wouldn't unless Tante spoke to her first and apologized for slapping her. She hoisted the tray higher and walked faster. She'd taken only two full steps when her legs nearly buckled beneath her. She stopped to regain her balance, but the world went wobbly as cooked custard. It spun around her as if it were playing ring-a-rosy with her at the center. Closing her eyes to stop the motion, she sank to her knees.

In the distance she heard porcelain shatter and the ringing clatter of metal dropped onto brick; she wondered if Tante Perte had dropped something in the cookhouse. She wondered why the sun had suddenly gone out like a snuffed lamp.

The sound of a spade cutting soil grew louder in her ears, and Tante Abeille's voice sang-spoke to the spade's rhythm. Beatrice opened her eyes to a sky at night. It was so cold that her breath hung in the air. An owl hooted. Beside her Tante was digging—shaping a large hole, longer than it was wide. She stopped to push the blade into a mound of loose dirt, and then dropped a cloth packet into the hole and made a series of complicated symbols over it with her fingers.

Beatrice tried to move but her limbs felt heavy and clumsy. She gasped at a sudden bolt of pain that streaked across her forehead. Tante Abeille stiffened and stopped the ritual over the grave. She turned and peered over her shoulder with caution, as if she'd been caught at something.

Tante's face was younger, and she frowned deeply at Beatrice. She drew a bottle from her waist pouch, took the stopper from it with her teeth, and squatted low. Gritty fingers pried open Beatrice's lips, and a thick, bitter potion drizzled into her mouth.

Choking and terrified, Beatrice struggled against the poison and the hands that forced it into her. Panic brought forth a burst of strength, and with the viciousness of a barn cat, she spat and clawed and shook her head. Something sharp and unforgiving cracked the side of her head, and she cried out at the new blaze of pain.

At the sound of her own shrill, frightened voice, her eyes flew open wide. Daylight again! How the light hurt; it pressed against her eyeballs like something solid. She could barely focus on the three faces clustered over her.

"Don't try and sit up just yet," Tante Perte said, worry trembling her voice.

Tante Las pressed a wet cloth to Beatrice's head. "You hit your skull when you fell. Got a knot near big as a hen's egg, you surely do."

Tante Abeille, holding a dipperful of water, said nothing. Even the tiniest word couldn't have squeezed past the grim, crimped line of her mouth—the same as in the dream. She held the dipper lower so that Beatrice could drink. But Beatrice turned her head away, unable to master her fear enough to take the offering. The faint, bitter taste of poison still clung to the back of her tongue.

For the remainder of the day Beatrice rested, though she swore she didn't need to. Her arguments fell on deaf ears. Tante Las swept the broken crockery from the whistler's path and took the damaged silver tray to the smith for repair. Tante Perte returned to the unending chores of the kitchen. But Tante Abeille decided the garden could wait while she sat watch over her niece.

Her chair complained as she rocked at the threshold of the cabin's open door and fanned herself while Beatrice lay atop her moss mattress. The throbbing song of cicadas wore on Beatrice's nerves, and she felt restless from the heat. Neither she nor Tante spoke, each waiting for the other.

She turned onto her belly, put her chin on her forearms, and regarded Tante carefully. Even though she reasoned the fall and the blow to her head had caused her to dream what she had, she felt ill at ease and suspicious. Especially after what Michie had said. So many who were close to Tante Abeille came to harm: Rosabel, then Grandmère Derora, then Maman Ara. Yet Tante was never sick, or hurt, and hardly seemed to age. Beatrice's stomach churned, and she rolled to face the wall beside her cot.

Tante Abeille finally broke the quiet. "How did you fall? Was the moss on the path slick, or did your toe hit an uneven brick?"

When Beatrice didn't answer quickly, Tante

clucked her tongue in annoyance. She fetched a cup. In it she crushed a plump rosehip and added some strips of black willow bark, and filled it with hot water. When it had steeped long enough she strained it with a spoon and drizzled in some honey and gave it to Bea. "Drink this."

Beatrice took it and put it to her lips, pretending to sip. Just the fragrance of the herb tea was enough to settle her a bit, and so she held it beneath her nose, breathing and saying nothing for a while. Then hesitantly, "When I hit my head I dreamed I saw you beside a grave."

Tante Abeille scuttled over and closed the door, then moved her chair beside Beatrice. "Did you know whose grave?" she whispered.

"Mine."

Tante flinched and quickly made the sign to avert evil. She chose her words carefully. "A grave mightn't be a grave at all in a dream. Things aren't always what they seem."

"What else can a grave be but what it is?"

"A door, a passageway, an entrance in, or a way out." Tante paused and tapped the center of her forehead. "A sign. A calling."

"A prophecy?" Beatrice countered, her tone accusing. In the same tone she demanded, "Where did you bury my grandmère when you took her from her coffin?"

Caught off guard, Tante Abeille blinked. She licked the dryness from her lips, gathering herself before she answered. "She rests at a place she chose for herself—I can't say where."

Beatrice put the untouched herb tea in Tante Abeille's hands and then turned away. Still as stone, she pretended to fall asleep, but her mind was fully awake. She drew the locket half from her pocket and worried it between her fingers.

I will find Grandmère's bones, she promised herself, and suddenly realized it would be so. Tante could not hide them from her much longer.

CHAPTER SEVEN

Metalwork

EATRICE took to sleeping beside the kitchen hearth on a pallet rather than return to her cot in Tante Abeille's cabin. Tante Perte and Tante Las allowed it, but not gladly, and for Abeille's sake they did not make Beatrice overly comfortable, in hopes she'd let go her grievance in favor of a softer bed. Each night they laid out a rag rug and gave her a thin blanket and told her to *dormez bien*—sleep well—before shutting themselves in their room.

Beatrice tried to sleep, but she'd somehow forgot the trick of it. Perhaps because her body wasn't weary at day's end the way it had been when she'd labored in the garden, but mainly because her mind wouldn't settle long enough for even a small dream to come. Given quiet and dark, her thoughts ran circles, and at the center was her vision of the grave and Tante Abeille. Other dreams faded quickly, but this one gripped her, becoming ever clearer and more real, as did her growing fear of revisiting it. Her desire to run from it overwhelmed her wanting to understand it.

After a week of frustrating restlessness, she could take it no more. Thinking it would be better to walk in the dark than to lie still and stare into it, she slipped outside with her blanket wrapped about her bare shoulders like a cape.

How changed the world looks in moonlight, she thought. Things familiar and known to her had shifted and seemed strange, like an old dress put on inside out and backward. Crickets and toads sang to the stars, but fell silent as she passed by, wandering the paths she had always traveled.

The garden's bowers and stalks and vines had turned into slump-shouldered beasts and rawboned haints in the dark. The maison appeared shadowy and moon-dappled, its walls softened by the feathery fronds of climbing wisteria that reached to the slate roof. Down the lane, the double row of cabins in the quarter yawned with dark and toothless maws rather than doors or windows.

In sighs and moans, the sounds of sleep drifted from inside, along with the smells of stale pork grease and dirty chamber pots. She crept close to one cabin and listened to the snores and mumbles of dreamers through the cloth tacked over the windows in place of glass. The woman inside was Kerel's older sister, Zina, who scolded her little son whenever she caught him smiling at Beatrice.

On impulse Beatrice pointed her fingers and put them atop her head, then stuck her tongue out and waggled it at the window. She drew a *vever* in the dirt, one she'd seen Tante Abeille drew with ash: a coffin shape topped by a cross. She didn't know the meaning of it, but wanted Zina to find it and think it a hex symbol. Let her fret and worry, Beatrice thought, covering her mouth to stifle a laugh.

She stole through the quarter as quiet as a ghostly *zombie*. No one scowled at her, or shooed her away, or crossed their fingers in her direction. There was no tante watching over her, no overseer telling her to work. So long as she didn't leave the bounds of Michie's farm, she could do what pleased her most, and go wherever her feet took her. This was what it was like to feel free. Her breath caught in her throat at the thought.

She stole up the carriage lane, darting from behind the trunk of one live oak to hide behind the next. She climbed the levee and stood atop it gazing out at the river. Maman had tried to drown in it.

The wide, oily water stretched out nearly as wide as the cane fields, but then she'd never seen where the cane ended in forest, just as she'd never walked any distance along the levee beside the river. She could only guess which stretched widest or farthest. Barges and steamboats came from somewhere upriver and took sugar somewhere down it, but just how far or wide the world stretched away from Rillieux Plantation she couldn't imagine beyond the knowing of place names: Orléans, Louisián, America, France, Afrik, Ayti.

To think of lands beyond the cane and the river kindled a fire behind her breastbone—a yearning she couldn't allow herself to think about. Night altered truth. That's why the most vivid dreams came at night. Nightmares could stick in your mind like a splinter, but trying to hold tight to a good dream was as impossible as gathering moonbeams. Beatrice held her palms open, letting the moonlight fill them, and then quickly closed her fingers. When she opened her hands again, they were empty.

✼ ✼ ✼

Beatrice had scarcely fallen asleep when Tante Las touched her on the shoulder and said, "You've slept late, *piti*. Up now and fetch a kettle of water from the cistern and some eggs from the chicken house."

She pushed herself up from her pallet and rubbed the sleep dust from her eyes. Then she quickly added wood to the embers in the hearth, something she usually did before Perte and Las rose in the morning.

Outside it was a gray-lit morn, rosy at the edges. The cistern ran clear water without green clots to skim out, and the hens chuckled and let her empty their nest boxes of eggs without a fuss. When she returned, Tante Perte took them and said, "Run to the smith's and see if he's yet fixed the bends in that tray you dropped."

Beatrice scowled. She and Kerel hadn't crossed paths since she'd left the dead rats in his gloves. "But, Tante, it's already so late . . ."

"Then hurry back," Tante Perte insisted without letting Beatrice finish. She turned and pushed her hands into the round of pastry dough resting on the worktable, a sign that there would be no further arguments.

But there was no hurry in Beatrice, only dread at having to face Kerel sooner than she wanted. She slowed further as she drew near the blacksmith shop, and wondered at the quiet. It was early morning, but she'd thought to hear some sound of the day's work being readied: the crackle of fire in the forge chimney, the clink of tools being moved, the pump of a bellows. It was quiet but for the sound of murmured voices drifting from the small window of the shop's living quarters.

Beatrice crept to it and peeked through a tear in the cloth covering, much as she'd done during her night wanderings. The smith and Kerel sat side by side with their backs against the wall below the window. Between them lay a slate tile like those that covered the roof of the maison. The smith held a stick of charcoal in his fingers, and with it scratched a string of letters onto the tile. He gave the stick to Kerel, who repeated the pattern with his own hand below the smith's. Beatrice held her breath. Writing—just as Michie had done with his quill in the ledger book! She recognized the first and last of the letters, but none of the others. The smith pointed to each letter and made a noise, as did Kerel. They repeated the sounds faster so that the noises came together into a spoken word: *river.*

Where had they learned this trick? Reading was forbidden—unheard of in the quarter. But the smith had come from the island country of Ayti, and perhaps had learned it there. His first master, fearing a revolt on the island, had brought him to Louisián and sold him to Michie for a high price. Tante Abeille said the smith's skill at metalwork made him valuable. That skill—and his claim of a last name—made him a proud man. And he still carried something of Ayti in his blood—a constant fever that made him hard to master.

Tante said the first time he had run away, the dogs and the overseer had caught him before he had gotten far. He had lost an ear for his trouble. The second time he got farther, but not far enough. The overseer pressed a hot branding iron to his forehead as if it were the flank of a cow. That hadn't stopped him, and he tried running yet again, but his branded face made him easy to spot. A bounty hunter returned him for a reward.

Rather than risk a beating that might kill the smith, the overseer decided to hobble him as punishment. Four field hands gripped each arm and leg tight as they could and held the smith's foot on the big anvil. They crushed it with a hammer meant for iron. A crippled blacksmith could work the forge, but couldn't run again.

So far as Beatrice knew, he hadn't run again, and yet he didn't seem much sorry for himself or for what he'd done. Always the smith held his back straight and looked anybody in the eye no matter who it was: field hand, Tante Abeille, overseer, or Michie himself. He had no friends in the quarter, but no one dared call him a name other than his own, or cross him other than to say he was too bold for his own good luck, and too proud to know what his true place was in this world.

Beatrice slipped her hand inside her pocket and found the broken locket. She rubbed the smooth side on which letters had been etched, and strained to get a closer look at the letters on the slate. She mouthed the word the smith had written on it: *RIVER*. She whispered it, matching sound to each letter as Kerel had done.

The smith quickly swiped his forearm over the tile and pushed it beneath the mattress. He turned his head toward the window, listening. Where his ear should have been there was but a hole in his skull surrounded by a fleshy ridge—a lizard's ear. Beatrice ducked below the window and covered her mouth with her hand. They'd accuse her of being Michie's spy, and that was far worse than being called a witch.

She crept along the wall and circled the entire blacksmith shop before she approached the smith's door and knocked. Labored footsteps crossed the floor inside—skip then step, skip then step. The door swung open, and the scent of catfish fried in lard and stewed okra greeted her more warmly than the smith. His eyes were dark and hard as disks of burned sugar. The branded *R* on his forehead was distorted by a lumpish layered scar that reminded her of the pinkish meat found beneath the dusky skin of a ripe plum. He frowned, making the knotted flesh crease down the middle.

"*Sa ena?*" he asked. The words rolled from his tongue with the rhythm of Ayti, his Creole accented by cassava and bonnet pepper rather than Louisián's swamp-apple and cayenne.

"N-nothing is wrong," Beatrice stammered, looking away from his face and the twisted foot that peeked beneath his pant leg. "Tante Perte sent me for the tray."

Behind the smith, Kerel lingered in the shadows. An iron cage filled one corner of the small room. Perched within was a young grackle. It ruffled its green-black feathers and stared at her with bright golden eyes. Kerel reached in and gently stroked the creature's head so that it hunched down into its winged shoulders. Still it clacked its beak grumpily at her. "He is frightened of *hibou*," Kerel said, mocking.

The smith raised his hand in warning and spoke to Kerel without removing his gaze from Beatrice. "Fetch this girl what she's asking for." Then to Beatrice he added, "It's not so terrible a name to be called. Better to be an owl of the wood than a chicken in a fenced yard, eh?"

Beatrice bit her lips to keep from smiling as Kerel pushed past her. He gave her shoulder a knock, but before she toppled, the smith caught her. His callused fingers closed on her wrist as tight as a leather whip, and she put her free hand to his chest to steady herself. His heart beat beneath her palm— a single beat that rattled her bones and thundered in her ears. Time moved slowly, winding down as it did during a vision, or a finding. Then it stopped and flowed backward, gaining speed and strength.

Beatrice resisted the current until her strength failed. Time pulled her under, swept her away in a blur. When she opened her eyes again, she was still in the blacksmith's shop. Only now both her arms were stretched above her head, her wrists bound together by a leather harness that had been strung over a roof beam. She dangled with her toes scarcely touching the dirt. Flames crackled in the firebox at the back of the raised hearth. The overseer was feeding it dried cane pulp and sticks of wood, and another man worked the bellows so that the fire burned hot and fierce inside the forge and gave off smoke that smelled like syrup candy. Her mouth watered at the scent of sweet caramel.

A crowd gathered, but they hung back, frightened. To one side, Tante Perte and Tante Las held each other. Beside them Tante Abeille held the hand of a little girl Beatrice didn't know. In a moment the overseer pulled an iron from the embers in the firebox. The backward letter *R* at its tip glowed yellow-orange. He held it in front of Beatrice's face. The sudden heat made her flinch, but she could not look away from the little girl's wide eyes.

Most in the crowd raised their hands to stop from seeing, some raised eyes toward heaven and cried out; some looked away or at the ground and cried tears. But the little girl's eyes remained fixed on Beatrice's, unblinking and steady, and Beatrice gazed into the girl's unwavering, terrified face and could see what she saw: the smith dangling from the rafters by his wrists. And then the iron touched his forehead so that the smell of roasting meat mingled with that of the burning cane pulp. The smith opened his mouth to scream, and it was Beatrice's own mouth opening—a hot pink bloom of a mouth that showed every sharp white tooth. It was her pain and not her pain. She both watched and felt.

Pain did not drive the smith's scream, she understood, but a fury hotter than the glowing iron. This was not the silly startled squawk of a hen bound for the cook's pot, but the wild cry of a tethered hawk who, given a chance, would sink its curved beak into the hands that fed him; who, given half a chance, would gnaw through leather or leg to escape again into a sky as blue as island seas.

Just as quickly as he'd caught her, the smith lessened his grip and Beatrice lost the moment. She yanked her hand free of him and rubbed her wrist, caught her breath. The smith's puckered scar had turned a deeper shade of red. It seemed a third eye, a flesh-eye, maybe a demon's eye. The spot where Beatrice thought the iron had touched her face tingled. She put her fingers there and found but her own smooth skin.

The smith tapped the hardened knot between his brows. "Price of a dream and worth it. Reminds me I flew once, till they clipped my wings. I am more than one of Michie's yardbirds."

"But they hung you up by your wrists and made everyone watch!"

The smith tilted his head to one side. "Happened when your *maman* was younger than you are now. How do you know?"

Beatrice felt a cold trickle of sweat trace the nape of her neck. Even if she wanted to explain, she couldn't. "Tante told me what happened," she lied.

"Your *maman* saw them burn me. I remember her eyes—green as bottle glass jes' like yours. Every eye turned away but hers."

Beatrice's felt as though he'd punched her with his fist and knocked the breath from her. Her dress felt damp beneath the arms. She was quite certain she'd seen a memory. Had the smith forced it on her, or had it come from Maman? But could memory pass from a mother to a baby? Did old hurts and sadnesses and terrors pile up inside each new life until the burden grew too heavy, until you began to crave the river bottom?

"Where is Kerel with that tray?" Beatrice asked, wanting to be away from the smith and his scar.

"I knew your *popa* better than your *maman*. He called me by my true name, Monsieur Gú."

Beatrice said nothing, and the smith took her silence to mean she didn't know the old lore. He told her the same story Tante Abeille had told of Gú, the first blacksmith. How he stole fire from the sun and took metal ore from the earth and forged people and animals and plants to live in Afrik when it was new and lifeless. What the smith didn't guess was that Tante sometimes stopped her work in the garden to listen to him beating out a rhythm with his hammer on the anvil, a ringing metal-on-metal sort of music, a clanging drumbeat. Echo of Afrik, she called it and said *loa* gathered at the sound of it.

"Did you choose that name?" Beatrice asked.

"The name chose me and I accepted." The smith brought his fist to the center of his chest and tapped his knuckles on his breastbone. "To decide who you are and what you are is a great power. No one can truly own me if I already own myself, eh?"

Beatrice nodded to humor him. For once she was grateful to see Kerel. He had the tray in hand, and the smith took it, wanting to show Beatrice his skill in removing every dent and in straightening perfectly the bent handle. In his rough hands the newly polished silver glimmered like mirrored glass, like moonlit water, or Mawu's face.

"*Merci,*" Beatrice said, rudely snatching the tray from the smith in her haste to be going.

"Time to fly, *hibou?*" Kerel asked. He snorted at his own joke, and it sent fresh venom through Beatrice's veins. Oh, but he wouldn't smirk if he knew she'd seen him reading. The overseer would wipe the smile off Kerel's fire-singed face when he found out. A rooster who crowed once too often usually ended up in the stew pot.

CHAPTER EIGHT

Bees

ABEILLE did not look up as Beatrice passed by the garden, but she stopped her work to listen to the song the girl was humming. It was *Marasa Élo*, the hymn that Ara had sung for Beatrice on the day she'd filled the thimble with tears. It was a mournful song, but in place of sadness, it filled Abeille with the hope that Beatrice had embraced some of the old lore of Afrik.

Beatrice, like Ara, was *sang mêlé*—of mixed

blood—and Abeille had decided it was the blood not of Afrik that had swayed both of them away from Mawu. She'd done all she could to keep Beatrice on the right path. But no matter the tales she told her, or the prayers she prayed, or the offerings she made on the girl's behalf, Beatrice wanted to veer in the wrong direction. Now, to hear her humming the twins' hymn lifted Abeille's spirits and gave her fresh resolve.

Though Beatrice still wouldn't speak to her beyond courtesy, she knew something of what was happening inside the maison. It wasn't difficult for a honeybee to fly through an open door, or ride inside atop Beatrice's shoulder or hide in the folds of her *tignon*. So long as they weren't discovered and swatted, the scouts told Abeille as best they could what they saw.

The old drone was courting the young queen, they said, which alarmed Abeille. But she reminded herself that bees expressed themselves in the very simplest terms, based only on what they understood of the natural world. *Courting,* to them, was any action by a drone that made him seem favorable or attractive.

"How do you know he is courting the young one?" she'd asked them.

He gives her sweets. Her mouth curls whenever he speaks. He says what is tracked on the bundled leaves.

The first two points were clear enough, but Abeille had puzzled about the last for a while before she concluded the bees had seen Reynard reading to Beatrice from a book. But what could be made of their report that the young queen kept a shiny bit of moonlight hidden in her pouch?

They all reported that Beatrice had begun to change in an unseen and unexplainable way, and Abeille trusted them in this belief. Bees had a mysterious sense and knowing within them; a hive was very like one body with many souls. A hive of bees recognized each of its souls the way a body knew each part of itself—that hand and fingers belonged to it while a stone held in that hand didn't. From her life in the garden with Abeille, the bees knew Beatrice and felt her restlessness. She'd always smelled of pollen and soil, but now her hair smelled more of river water, and her skin felt warmer, as if she were fighting a fever.

To Abeille it meant that Mawu was at work in the girl, just as it had happened to herself and Derora when they were girls of twelve. Abeille remembered noticing first that the air had different flavors that changed with the seasons: floral sweet in spring, rich and fruity in summer, musky in autumn, bland as egg white in winter. Sometimes, out of nowhere, bees would swarm around her and sting anyone nearby, yet leave her unhurt. Before she learned to speak to the swarm and keep them at bay, everyone in the quarter began to call her *hibou*-witch and keep their distance from her and Derora.

With Derora there had first been dark dreams and blinding visions that hurt her eyes; nothing she could control. But she'd learned in time. Her sight was always forward, never backward, and never farther than a few days ahead. She found her vision showed what was likely, but not absolute. Seeing was water-linked, and she compared the visions to heavy fog—moisture that seemed solid but could be shifted by breath or movement. Water was flexible in form until it froze solid; the future was liquid until the freezing moment it became the past.

Ara never had faith in this truth. To her, every forward glimpse was a fatal prophecy, hopelessly unavoidable. She could never believe in unseen possibilities, and so every vision came about just as she'd imagined it. This was why she had fought against her birthright, and called her gift a curse. But in hating her birthright, she'd hated herself. There was no greater curse than that.

Abeille sighed. She closed her eyes and listened to her bees at their work. Late summer now and they were in a frenzy to gather nectar from the last of the flowers. The rose bower and wisteria vine were alive with them during the day, and the box hives in the pasture vibrated with a mechanical hum at night from the tireless beating of millions of wings. She could hear them inside her cabin with the door closed, and even in her sleep. The sound plucked at her heart and made her soul restless. It told her she had little time left. Ripples from a stone cast long ago would soon reach the shore at her feet.

She opened her eyes again and watched Beatrice disappear inside the maison, humming softly, with a honeybee trailing close behind her. The foolish *lapin* who trusted old man *krokodi* would soon disappear behind his teeth and end up in his belly.

Abeille spat in the direction of the maison. Beatrice needed to be taught and guided. She needed to hear more of the old songs and stories of Afrik—words held in heart and mind and reborn with each new telling. Not those stale words captured in Michie's books—dried-up old ink stains on paper. Bah!

Beatrice was almost thirteen years old. She needed her grandmère Derora.

Beatrice could not help but notice Tante Abeille each time she passed by the garden, and each time she felt like a joint of sugarcane that had been split from end to end. One part of her wanted to forget their argument and to hear Tante ramble on again about weather, and roses, and the gossip of honeybees. She missed leaning against Tante's knobbed knees in the evening and listening to the lore or songs of Afrik while the old woman's fingers worked her hair into neat plaits.

Seeing what had become of the beautiful garden scoured Beatrice's heart. Tante worked alone now, and the beds had quickly grown tatty with stinging nettles, bindweed, poison ivy, and cat-briar. Tante seemed untended as well—her bones sharper, her clothes loose as a scarecrow's, her hair whiter, and every movement stiff and slow.

But the stronger half of Beatrice nursed a

smoldering anger, and looked for new fuel. She passed by the garden and felt Tante glare with disapproval at her back. She never voiced her ire, but Beatrice sensed it, so scorching hot that she smelled her hair burning; like thrown stones it bruised her ribs. Unspoken words filled the silence between them: *Fool. Child. Michie's pet.*

"She is jealous," Beatrice told herself. "Jealous of me like she was of Grandmère."

Just inside the back door she heard a low buzz and turned to shoo a bee outside. It sped upward toward the ceiling and disappeared. Michie hated bees above every creature, even vipers. His body reacted so violently to bee venom that he feared he'd die if ever he were stung again. One or two managed to follow her through the door nearly every day, hard as she tried to keep them out. She caught them when she could, and cupping them in her bare hands, tossed them outside where they belonged. But Michie had no mercy and dispatched them with a swatter or a book.

Beatrice searched for the errant bee while she walked down the hall to the study. Just as she reached the door she heard a loud *thwack* followed by muttered curses. "Scoundrels! That's the second to wander in here today."

Michie's scowl softened when he saw Beatrice. He pointed to a little curled body lying on the carpet, and Beatrice bent to pluck up the bee. She saw that its sting-end still pulsed with life. Maybe he'd only knocked it senseless and not killed it, poor thing. She dropped it in her pocket with the broken locket, in hopes it would recover.

"If I'd never been stung I would be just as fearless as you with them," he said, and opened the small book he'd used as a weapon. From it he began reading aloud while she straightened the room. This had become his habit; sometimes he read from a book of Scripture, or another that contained what she called singing words and he called poetry, or from one of Mamzelle Rosabel's books of fairy stories.

For a small time of the day, with the book stories surrounding them, and the garden and the quarter and the fields shut away and forgotten, she felt as if she belonged *with* Michie Reynard—not *to* him. In a short time, she'd grown fond of working inside the grande maison, where Michie Reynard read to her alone.

The words from his books sounded grand, and so different from Tante Abeille's animal tales of Compair Lapin and Compair Bouki, who were the rabbit and the fool; or the stories of the trickster spider; or the serpent god, Danbala, who held the world tight in his coils.

On one table in the study there was a ball no bigger than a melon mounted on a spindle that allowed the ball to twirl. Michie called the thing a globe and said it was a rounded map of the world entire. To see all the world made so small that it fit on a tabletop disappointed Beatrice, and the shape of it confounded her. She'd always thought of the world as stretching out and out, not round and round.

Michie had a large book that contained flat-tened maps of the land too, which seemed far more sensible to her than the globe. He had shown her a page that contained all of Louisián, and laughed when she said it looked to her like snake tracks and bird blots on sand. He pointed to the blots and said, "These are lakes." Of the largest snake track he said, "This is a river."

When he'd said *river* Beatrice felt her heart gain speed. Beside the squiggled line was the word the smith had written on the roof slate: RIVER. To see it written inside a book, and to recognize it, thrilled and terrified her. "Old Devil River?"

"*Oui*, the very same," he had answered, then closed Louisián inside the volume and returned it to the shelf.

Beatrice worked slowly, wanting to draw out longer this morning reading time. As she ran her dust rag over the spines of the shelved books, she found the one with the maps and thought of Kerel. What trouble he and the smith would have if

Michie knew they had knowledge of words and could open to a page and read it just as he did. It seemed a better talent than finding buttons and needles, but not as useful. There were no books in the quarter to read, no way to get them, and even if you could, it was strictly forbidden. But not forbidden everywhere in the world, or the smith wouldn't have learned it. She trailed the rag over the globe so that it spun slowly.

Michie had stopped reading, and she turned to find him studying her intently. He said, "From behind, you are Derora." His voice was wheezy from the effort of reading aloud, and tinged with grief. More and more often he spoke of Grandmère when Beatrice was with him, and he called her Derora more often than her own name. She didn't dare correct him—and it pleased her.

Beatrice wondered if there was a spell at work on the maison. Some sort of hex that caused Grandmère's presence to linger in the air like pipe smoke; a longing, probing sort of presence that Beatrice could not understand beyond knowing that it belonged to both her and Michie. It was as if a spider's thread connected them and drew them toward each other.

Reynard wondered if the tenderness he so quickly felt toward Beatrice would have happened had she not favored Derora in appearance. He regretted that he hadn't been tender with Derora in the end, but he'd been angry—and afraid of her. He could admit that to himself after all this time, if not to anyone else.

Beatrice felt more comfortable with him each day; he could see it. She turned now from her dusting to see why he'd stopped reading and caught him staring. She rewarded him with a shy smile that made his breath hitch in his throat. He'd not felt such a thing in many years. He'd never felt it for Ara, because her birth had killed Derora. He'd told Beatrice the old rumor of the poisoning only to cast a shadow over Abeille, and it had worked. *Non,* it was Ara who'd killed Derora. But he could forgive Ara now. She'd given him Beatrice.

The girl tucked her dust rag in the waistband of her skirt. "You look flushed, Michie. Would you like something to drink?"

"*Oui,*" he said, "a glass of wine."

She poured it carefully and brought it to him, and fussed over him in an agreeable way. Without being asked, she set about fanning him until he was comfortable.

He didn't like to think of her sleeping on the floor of the cookhouse, nor did he wish her to move back into the cabin with Abeille. The old crone had done her job in raising the girl and protecting her. Beatrice no longer belonged in the quarter. He wanted her closer to him.

He thought of the empty room upstairs that had been Rosabel's, and then Derora's. It overlooked the garden and had a fine view of the river. She could stand at the window and gaze out just as the princess had from the castle tower in the fairy story he'd read aloud yesterday.

"Beatrice, did you like the story of Persinette?" he asked.

She pursed her mouth and glanced toward the garden. "*Oui*, but not the witch."

"Persinette escaped the old witch in the end. Princesses in fairy stories always do. Goodness always prevails."

Beatrice belonged in dresses the color of butterfly wings, he thought to himself. Not dull homespun cloth. He pictured her in slick rustling silk, green to match her eyes; her hair swept back and held with tortoiseshell combs or jewels. She needn't hide her hair beneath a slave's plain *tignon* any longer. She was nearly thirteen years old. Time to hire a governess to teach her proper manners, proper French, all the social graces a young lady need know. Perhaps he'd host a grand fête following harvest this year and invite all the families of *qualité* in the parish; no expense spared. Beatrice in her new glory would be the most splendid of all the ladies—the jewel of Maison Rillieux.

"Beatrice, there is a room upstairs I want you to see," he said, trying to quell the excitement in his voice. His strength had so dwindled that raising himself from his chair was difficult. He rocked forward and back trying to throw himself into standing, not wanting to ask for assistance.

But Beatrice offered her hand to him. "Let me steady you," she said gently. And without hesitation, he accepted.

CHAPTER NINE

Briar

ICHIE Reynard unlocked a door on the second floor and threw it open. "It needs freshening," he apologized. "I've not opened it in a long while, but you'll put it in order soon enough."

The room was as large as Tante Abeille's cabin in the quarter. A fringed needlepoint rug of mossy green lay upon the dusty cypress floorboards. Smooth linens embroidered with a garden of flowers dressed a carved wooden bed topped with a feather mattress and a net canopy. A tapestry chair sat before the room's fireplace. Fine lace hung at the two windows. A silver mirror glimmered over the wooden bath table with its porcelain basin and pitcher, and crystal candlesticks sat atop a little table gilded with gold.

The luxury left her speechless. She hung back, afraid to touch anything. "This was Mamzelle Rosabel's room?"

"*Oui*," he answered, pleased at her reaction. He thought it best not to mention it had last been Derora's.

He pointed her to a window that looked out over the alley of oaks that led to the river road, and beside it the levee, and below that the boat landing that jutted into the river. The shadows of passing clouds mottled the water, sliding over its surface with the barges and a lone paddlewheel boat.

The second window looked out at the garden, divided within its walls by brick paths, and Tante Abeille bent over some task in a bed. Beside the garden was the cookhouse. And when she peered slantwise she could see a portion of the quarter and the blacksmith's shop and the sugarhouse at the nearest edge of the cane fields.

"You like the room?" he asked.

"*Oui*, it's beautiful!" She drew her finger over the surface of a table and inspected the line left in the dust. "How soon will your guests be arriving?"

"Guests?" He smiled and shook his head. "No guests, *cher*. This is your room now."

Beatrice put her hands in her apron pockets so that Michie wouldn't see them shaking. "Mine? Can't I stay with Tante Las and Tante Perte?"

He stiffened. "You said you liked the room!"

"*Mais oui!* But I help them . . ."

"Damn them!" His cheeks burned with color. He worked his mouth beneath his mustache before he continued in a more controlled tone. "Someone else can help in the kitchen. They'll manage without you. You have until the morrow to settle yourself here with me."

Beatrice opened her mouth to plead. But there was no humor in Michie's face, nothing but hard resolve.

The stunned honeybee Beatrice had earlier dropped in her pocket awoke from its stupor and buzzed irritably against her fingertip. It nipped her with its pincer mouth, but didn't sting. As soon as Michie left her alone, she opened the window overlooking the garden and released it.

It flew downward toward the rose arbor with the speed of a hailstone and disappeared among the blossoms.

It was too hot to sleep near the kitchen hearth with its smoldering embers. Beatrice dragged the rug and her blanket to the threshold of the door. She opened it to let in the breeze. Moonlight splashed over the boards of the floor like dry, silver-blue water. Mawu was on the wax—plump by a half but not yet fully round.

Beatrice tried to imagine what it would be like

to sleep inside the maison so near—too near—Michie Reynard. And him so impulsive and odd of late, you couldn't be sure what he'd do or ask anymore.

Certainly a feather bed would be more comfortable than the cookhouse floor or her cot in Tante Abeille's cabin. And the green rug would feel nice beneath her feet. Glass windows would shut out cold damp weather better than cloth screens and shutters.

Glass windows . . . She sat up, startled by a sudden thought. Shaking.

In the reflection of the windows from the garden, she'd seen herself inside the maison, imagined herself belonging there, and now it was happening. Had she glimpsed what was always coming, or cast some sort of spell to cause it into being?

Tante Abeille would know. Maybe she'd known all along and said nothing!

Without bothering to dress, Beatrice slipped out into the dark and headed for Tante Abeille's cabin. She hesitated on the porch, unsure of whether to walk in or knock on the door as if she were an uninvited guest. As if the cabin had never once been her home. She did both, knocking as she opened the door a crack. "Tante," she whispered. "Tante, please, can I come in?"

Silence.

She pushed the door open halfway and peered around. "Tante? I need to talk to you . . ."

The single room was dark and very still. The shutters were drawn against the outside so that the air felt close and stuffy. She couldn't hear the old woman's rattling snore. Afraid of what she would find, Beatrice felt her way across the floor to Tante Abeille's bed. She put her hand atop the rumpled blanket expecting the worst, her heart in her throat. But the bed was empty. Faint with relief, Beatrice sat on the edge and waited for Tante Abeille to return.

She waited long and began to wonder and worry anew. A thin streamer of moonlight seeped in at the edge of the shuttered window, and she played her hand in and out of it at a regular pace so that it flashed over her palm in a rhythm of slow blinking that calmed her. She thought only of Tante Abeille, and her mind wandered forward as if following a thread through a tunnel. She recognized the sensation. This was finding. In her excitement she nearly lost her hold on the thread.

With new determination, she focused and followed through the tunnel. Near the end she saw pinpoints of flickering light that seemed to float in a row midair. She heard the whirring hum of machinery like a rice thresher, and Tante Abeille's voice rise and fall. She tried to draw closer but couldn't without letting go the thread. Her eyes felt dry with staring and her head had begun to throb, but she strained to see more. Black specks crisscrossed her vision, increasing in number and spinning about her until she felt dizzy. The hum of the thresher was deafening—and familiar. Bees in the garden, but much louder, and Tante calling her name: *Beatrice. Beatrice.*

Beatrice blinked and fell back onto Tante Abeille's cot, gasping air, faint for having held her breath too long. Hives. Tante was in the pasture with the hives. Something was wrong.

Beatrice stumbled to her feet and ran, each footfall a jolt to her pounding head. She passed by the last tumbledown cabin in the quarter, hurried by the outhouses that served it, and turned away from the cane fields. She ducked beneath a barbed, wooden fence that coiled about the pasture like a bramble hedge. Metal briars reached out to catch at her hair and her skin as she passed beneath the top rail. She pulled the edge of her cotton shift free from a nail and pushed forward into the shorn field.

Massive fork-heaped mounds of cut grass loomed up from the stubbly ground like great bee skeps, each large enough to hold a colony of honeybees many millions strong. Night creatures skittered away before her, ducked into the mounds, clambered over the arch of her bare foot. And up above her, the chirping sound of feeding bats faded in and out and in again.

She crossed herself against evil, touching her forehead, heart, and then each shoulder. She hurried from hay mound to hay mound, moving closer to the hives and the whirring sound of swarming bees. Sweat dampened her cotton slip so that it clung to her body like a second skin. The droning in her ears grew louder, and she paused behind the final mound listening to the agitated sound of them. And in it, faintly, she heard her name again.

Gathering her courage, she slid around the great curve of sweet-smelling grass. It was just as she'd seen it. A row of flickering candles lined the fence rail. The dancing flames appeared to float midair in the dark while wax bled down over the boards in dripping rivulets. The hives—rough wood boxes set on stumps one beside the other in a long row—seemed a miniature version of the quarter. Attracted by the candlelight, a storm of honeybees spun in a black cloud, manic and whining so feverishly that the air felt aquiver with sound.

Bea's rib bones strummed. Thoughts rattled inside her aching head like seeds in a gourd—like an *asson*. In the midst of the storm of bees, Tante Abeille shook the sacred rattle, spinning and shimmying, her arms raised toward the glowing moon. She was barely visible amid the whirlwind of a million beating wings and half-million velvet bodies. And below the living cloud, her gnarled feet hung at a low hover, her toes dipping now and again to brush tips against the dirt. The bees worked to lift her as if she were a brown husk, an old beetle's shell, an empty pod and not a woman at all. No one Beatrice recognized, or had ever known.

Tante chanted strange words, punctuated by Beatrice's name, and Derora's. Beatrice stood transfixed. Tante hadn't been calling for help at all, she was calling Grandmère's spirit back from the dead. She was working a *wanga* spell. To call a soul

from death was black-magiic sorcery of the worst
kind. Beatrice cried out and quickly made the gesture to avert evil and turn it back on itself. The
sharp smell of vinegar and almond boiled out
toward her, and the bees roiled with greater agita-
tion. She felt their rage, and recognized the scent of
a hive attacked.

Turning, she ran blindly, weaving between the
piles of grass, mindless of the stones that bruised
her feet. At the barbed fence, she flung herself
through the slats, misjudged, and felt a nail rip
through her slip and furrow a long gash between
her shoulder blades. She paid it no mind. Her only
thought was that she must run faster and not look
back until she reached a safe place.

Dawn light filtered pinkly through Beatrice's eyelids but she did not open them. She lay still and
listened. Birds chirruped, a rooster crowed, and
honeybees hummed about the rose arbor. Not
angrily as they had the night before, but with

excitement. The ground clutter rustled beneath Beatrice as she stirred to sitting. Pain burned across her shoulder blades where the barbed fence had gouged her. An inky patch of dried blood where she'd lain at the base of the rose arbor told her the cut had bled a good bit during the night. Her cotton shift was stiff as bark and plastered to the wound.

But it wasn't pain that caught her breath in her throat. It was the rose.

Nothing about the great white rose looked as it had the night before when she'd sheltered beneath it. Overnight, graceful, arching stems and fluttering leaves had become a wild, rambling briar. Thick canes twisted up like sapling trees and bowed beneath the weight of thousands of juice-heavy berries the size of her thumb and the color of strong wine. Starry white flowers burst, out of season, from new shoots that twined together like serpents. Inside the green hollow there was hardly room enough to stand above a crouch, or to stretch out full length in any direction.

"Tante Abeille!" Beatrice wailed. "She has fixed me in here."

Beatrice kneeled inside the briar hollow like a chick in a green egg, her hands knotted in her lap, listening for the sound of Tante at work. But she heard nothing. By the strength of the light she could tell that the earliest part of the morning had passed by. Tante Las and Tante Perte would wonder where she was.

In frustration, she shoved her hand into the briar, hoping to make a way out. Thorns ripped into her knuckles; beads of blood sprang up like red embroidery stitches, like the thin lines on the maps in Michie's library. She cradled her wounded hand in the skirt of her shift and sobbed angrily.

"Let me out!" she screamed. "Tante Las! Tante Perte! Someone!" She yelled until her throat felt raw.

CHAPTER TEN

Locket

T ANTE PERTE'S eyes were dim, but her ears were keen enough to hear Beatrice's cries for help. Tante Las was the one to hunt for her and find her trapped within the briar. Dense as the briar was, a sharp cane knife would make short work of it, she assured Beatrice. All the blades were with the blacksmith who was readying them for the coming harvest, but she would go and fetch one. When Tante Las returned, she brought the knife with her, and Kerel to do the cutting.

Thorny canes fell away until there was a gap

large enough for him to peer through at Beatrice. She set her chin and glared up at him furiously, expecting the usual cruel name or taunt. But he held his tongue. His browless, heat-scoured face flicked from glowering annoyance to sudden surprise and then confused embarrassment. He averted his eyes from her, before he resumed hacking at the briar with great intensity.

Puzzled, Beatrice glanced down at herself. Loose petals and leaves had sifted over her bare arms and she brushed them away. *Zut!* No wonder he'd looked away: she was indecent! She wore only a thin cotton slip that had fallen from her shoulders and her hair was loose and uncovered! Mortified, she quickly turned her back to him, drew her bare legs beneath her, and covered her chest with her hands.

After a while he cleared his throat and said, "You can crawl out now, I think there's space enough."

"Turn around and close your eyes!" she yelped over her shoulder. "Or—or go away!" He'd seen her nearly naked, but he'd not have the satisfaction of watching her crawl past him in the dirt. She'd been humiliated enough without adding that to it.

"You're welcome," he said curtly.

Beatrice waited until Tante Las had thanked him and his footsteps had moved down the path, and the garden gate creaked open and then closed. As soon as she emerged, Tante Las gathered her up and cried, "You are hurt at your wing spots, *piti!*" She touched the cut place between Bea's shoulders and clucked her tongue. "It's deep, but Perte will put a balm on it. It'll heal."

"Tante Abeille . . ." Beatrice began in a rush, but Tante Las held a finger to her lips. Her expression became grave. "Quiet until we are in the kitchen."

Tante Perte looked as grim as Tante Las. She folded Beatrice in a pillowy embrace and whispered, "Praise! I feared you'd gone after Abeille when we didn't find you this morning."

"She's run off!" Tante Las blurted, her voice anxious and raspy.

"How do you know?"

"Last night you were sad about moving into the maison. Then this morning we found your dress but not you, and I hoped you'd decided to go home to Abeille. Maybe you'd spent your last night in your own cot. So I went there to take your dress to you, and saw that neither cot had been slept in." She paused, choosing her next words. "The emptiness seemed final: no spirit, no breath, no life. You know what it is to look at an empty cicada husk—you can see what was, but 'tisn't and never again will be. That's the feel of Abeille's cabin."

Tante Perte placed a small bundle on the table: Tante Abeille's *tignon*, knotted like a package. "While you were with Michie yesterday, she came here and said give you this when you woke this morning but not before. She said keep it secret from the old man."

Beatrice took it and undid the knots, and unfolded the square of cloth to reveal half of an oval locket strung on a thin silver chain. Though broken at the hinge, the jewel's clasp was still intact—a tiny silver bee. Beatrice fetched from her apron pocket the locket face she'd found in the garden. When she laid the face atop the charm on the chain, it fit perfectly: the little bee snapped into place atop a silver bud on the face, hiding the scrolled words within the halves.

"It must have belonged to Mamzelle Rosabel," Tante Perte said.

Tante Las agreed, but seemed doubtful. "Could've wore it one day in the garden and broke it at the hinge, I suppose. Without the face piece it would've been ruined, so she might've gave it to Abeille."

"Mamzelle was very fond of Abeille," Tante Perte insisted. "Abeille wasn't afraid to stand Michie down. She was Mamzelle's protector."

Beatrice couldn't remember Tante ever wearing the locket. Probably much too fancy and far too French for her taste. Beatrice circled it around her neck. The metal was so cold it stung her skin, and did not warm quickly. Thin as it was, the chain felt ponderously heavy, as if made of thick iron links. But as soon as the chilled metal grew warm against her skin, she'd not wanted to take it off.

Later in the afternoon Beatrice led the overseer down the hallway to Michie's study. He'd found Tante Abeille's *asson* near the hives and brought it with him. The man's appearance reminded her of a sharp-ribbed hound. A pungent mixture of sweat-soaked clothing and rotten breath hung about him in a vapor. The snake bones in the *asson* rattled softly when he walked. He swiped his hat from his head with his free hand just outside the study door, but his hair had taken on the shape of the hat's crown.

"*Entrez,*" Michie barked when Beatrice knocked. The overseer ran his tongue over chapped lips, took a deep breath, and went inside.

Beatrice stayed in the hallway listening; nervously zipping the half-locket back and forth across its chain. The soft buzzing sound it made beneath her chin calmed her, but she dropped it to better hear what Michie and the overseer were saying. The man mumbled greetings, and then quickly launched into a blustering tirade. "You should have sent that woman to the cane fields when Madame died, Monsieur Rillieux. Or sold her long ago! You'll recall I did recommend it after her niece flung herself into the river."

"You did," Michie agreed, sighing, "but I am too softhearted."

The overseer shook the *asson* violently. "That's why you have me, Monsieur! I'll have a boy saddle my horse in a blink, and drag her back at the end of a long rope. She's old and on foot. She'll not have got very far."

Beatrice felt her stomach roil and her marrow turn to frost. A bell sounded from inside the study, but she didn't recognize it until it rang a second time, impatiently.

"Mon chagren!" she apologized, rushing in to see what Michie needed.

He smiled at her kindly and then said to the overseer, "Beatrice may know what's become of her old tante."

Beatrice thought of the hives and the storm of bees working to tug Tante Abeille from the ground. She stared at the *asson* in the overseer's hand. "*Non*, Michie," she said, "I don't know."

Michie drummed his fingers on his lips, then stood and took the ledger of names from its place on the shelf. He opened it to the page of names he'd shown Beatrice once before. He made a line with his pen through one of the names on the ledger and said, "Trouble has always followed on Abeille's heels. Let her take it somewhere else."

The overseer looked surprised. "Let her get away, Monsieur?"

"*Oui!* She's done us a favor." He touched the center of his chest. "And I haven't the heart that you do, as we both agree."

The overseer dipped his head in puzzled agreement and laid the *asson* on Reynard's desk. "Not much more work in her. Not enough to earn her keep. The cost to keep the old ones fed and clothed is more than they're worth to us. At least you can eat a hen that's stopped laying eggs." Chortling at his own wit, he excused himself.

Beatrice followed him down the hall. Outside the back door he turned and gave her an oily grin; mostly gums spiked in a random pattern of half-rotted teeth that testified to his habit of sucking sugar lumps. He let his gaze slide over Beatrice in a way that drew her skin up and made her cheeks burn with shame. "The old fox let your tante go for a reason," he said knowingly.

"Because he is kind," Beatrice answered with too much heat. "He is not like you!"

The overseer let out a barking laugh, then he settled his hat atop his head. "He gets what he wants. That's all I'm certain of."

Kerel's sister, Zina, was the new kitchen help, and had also taken on Beatrice's duties as housemaid.

With harvest approaching, she'd been glad to trade the harder work of the sugarhouse for work in the cookhouse with Tante Perte and Tante Las, who welcomed her as they welcomed everyone. And Beatrice knew they enjoyed watching after Zina's little son, Frey, but she wished someone else had been chosen to take her place. Anyone but Kerel's unfriendly sister. Anyone who didn't remind her of him and how he'd looked at her through the briar canes. "Your milk-twin," Tante had told her. "Jealous you took half of what belonged to him by right." Yet for that moment in the garden he had looked at her differently.

From her room inside the maison Beatrice watched smoke rise from the cookhouse chimney. Zina emerged from the kitchen with her arms laden by the lunch tray. Beatrice couldn't hear the tune she whistled, but Zina's mouth was pursed so that it looked like one of the darker berries on the wild bramble that had overtaken the garden in the days since Tante Abeille had disappeared.

Ye shall reap what ye sow was a Scripture verse Michie had read that morning. It was similar to a thing Tante Abeille had once said about how a life planted with spite grew nothing but nettles and cockleburs, briars and chokevine—an ugly thicket to live with. The briar was proof of Tante's spite. She'd used it to trap Beatrice, and now it wanted to eat Mamzelle's garden. It was unnatural in the way it had so quickly devoured the corner and now spilled outside the enclosure of the garden walls, wild and hungry and heaving with honeybees.

Beatrice found it unnerving. She tried to ignore it, but in truth she couldn't, because it wouldn't let her. When she came close to it, she felt it lean toward her ever so slightly, its leaves whispering strangely in her ears. And the bees flocked about in droves and clung to her in clots if she didn't wave her arms constantly and ridiculously. Tante Las said she looked like a goose trying to fly away. Especially in her new dress with its broad, fussy sleeves.

Because she couldn't risk bringing bees inside

the house, and because Michie panicked if she didn't come to him the first time he rang his infernal bell, she rarely ventured outside anymore. She raised the window and put her head out where she could better hear Zina's tuneful whistling, and to savor a breath of fresh air.

The silver half-locket slipped from Beatrice's dress collar and dangled from her neck, glinting in the sunshine. Zina looked up at the flash of light and furrowed her brows angrily when she found Beatrice watching her.

"Bonjou!" Beatrice called down, if only to annoy Zina all the more. "Make sure you don't let bees in the door this time. Michie hates them."

Within minutes, the bell rang from the study downstairs, and Beatrice sighed. Michie was calling her to lunch.

Beatrice hadn't gotten used to eating with him at every meal, or him instructing her in the rules of "eating like a lady," which seemed to involve eating very little, very quietly. She moved her veal around in its sauce and then nibbled at her bread.

Michie frowned. "Don't bite into it like a mule after an apple! Tear off a small bit with your fingers." He demonstrated the technique, though clumsily. The tremors in his hands had grown more pronounced. Bringing a bite of food from plate to mouth took great concentration; one hand supported the wrist of the hand that held the spoon. Still, more of his rice spilled in his lap than reached his lips. Of necessity he allowed Beatrice to cut his food, but his pride wouldn't allow her to feed him. Not yet.

After lunch she held the book steady for him as he read to her. He used his finger to follow along the lines of words now; to keep them from dancing on the page, he said. Beatrice had begun to see patterns of sound and symbol, and even recognize many of the short words. It made her hungry to know more. It made her envy Kerel for being taught by the smith. Without a doubt she begrudged that of him as much as he begrudged sharing his mother with her.

While Zina collected the lunch dishes, Beatrice saw her pause to look at the book Michie had left on the table. She wondered if Zina knew Kerel's secret. Was he teaching Zina everything the smith had taught him?—Zina, who had scolded her child for smiling at Beatrice, and who glared at her when Michie wasn't looking. The idea of Zina learning to read puckered Beatrice's mouth.

As soon as Michie settled in for an afternoon nap, Beatrice left him for the cookhouse. As she drew near it the sound of Zina and Tante Perte and Tante Las laughing merrily stung her. Zina had taken her place at the hearth so quickly and easily.

It took the group more than a moment to notice her because Tante Las was showing Zina's son, Frey, a game with a loop of string. She'd woven it between her fingers in the pattern of cat's whiskers and held it below her nose. *"Mouw!"* she cried, in a cat's voice, and the boy fell back giggling. He was the first to see Beatrice, and ran to Zina to hide his face in her skirts. Tante Perte and Tante

Las greeted Beatrice kindly, but with reserve. It felt as if a cold wind had blown through the kitchen and chilled the air.

Vexed, Beatrice smoothed the muslin skirt of her new green dress and raised her chin above the itchy lace collar. "Zina, can I speak with you?" she asked, knowing well that Zina couldn't refuse. Michie had told her she must answer to Beatrice as she would him, though she always scowled and sulked about it.

When they were outside Beatrice removed the locket face from inside the hidden pocket-slit at the side of her dress and held it so that the scrolled words showed. Zina glanced down and then raised one questioning brow.

"Do you know what it says?"

"Why would I?" Zina asked, clearly perturbed.

"Maybe if you looked at it longer."

Zina sighed heavily and studied the silver oval for half a second, and then shook her head. "*Non,* still can't. Is that all?"

"What about Kerel?"

Did a shadow of worry flick over Zina's face? Her voice was polite, but guarded. "He maybe could fix where it's broke," she answered. "Why don't you show it to him? He's coming up behind you."

Frey squealed and ran at Kerel as soon as he caught sight of him. Kerel dropped the two newly sharpened kitchen knives he'd brought and held his arms out to let the little boy leap at him from the doorway. But Zina plucked him up quickly and put him on her hip. She tipped her head at Beatrice. "She wondered who could help her with a broken locket—silver and very fancy. I said you might." A look passed between them.

With barely a glance at Beatrice, Kerel held out his hand. Beatrice hesitated, and then dropped the locket face in it, and took the chain from around her neck. "You can see the halves fit together, but the hinge is broken."

"Did Michie give it to you to go with that fine new dress?" Kerel asked. He was mocking her.

"*Non,* Tante Abeille did," Beatrice snapped.

Kerel nodded, but not so much in agreement as in disagreement. He held it out toward her. "I can't fix it, but you could give it to the smith."

"Why can't you take it to him for the lady, Kerel?" Zina piped in. Beatrice could hear that she was teasing him, and he gave his sister a withering glare for it. She lifted her brows innocently and ducked inside the kitchen with Tante Perte and Tante Las.

Kerel shrugged and looked at Beatrice aslant. He seemed nervous and it baffled her. She was the one who should be shy, not him. "If you want, I can take the locket to the shop," he mumbled, with his mouth turned down in a half-frown.

Beatrice looked back at the maison. Michie would be asleep a little while longer. "I'll go with you," she said, unwilling to trust him with anything so precious.

CHAPTER ELEVEN

Kerel

THEY WALKED in silence for a while with Kerel leading the way. He turned his head once to see that she was still behind him, but it was her bare feet he looked at rather than her face. "Don't you have shoes to go with your fancy new frock?" he asked.

She looked down at her naked toes poking from beneath the ruffled hem of her skirt. "I don't like the feel of a shoe on my foot," she answered defensively.

"I always thought shoes looked smothery,"

Kerel said. "What's it like to live in the maison?"

"Like wearing a shoe," Beatrice blurted, and then caught herself. "It's a little easier than living in the quarter, and much harder."

Kerel turned to look fully at her for the first time since the day in the rose briar. He stopped to let her come beside him. "The old man keeps you under his thumb, then?"

"*Oui.*" Beatrice narrowed her eyes at him. "You're being nice. Why?"

Kerel shrugged.

"I'm not Michie's spy, if you're worried. I'm not even supposed to be this far from the maison."

Kerel shrugged again and they walked on in silence, though side by side now.

At the shop the smith was working at sharpening the pile of cane knives, drawing the blades over oilstone and whetstone until the edges were sharp enough to divide a single hair or lop off a hand or cut and shuck an ocean's span of cane. Near the smith, the grackle's cage hung from a hook at the corner of the eaves, and it screeched when it caught sight of Kerel and Beatrice. The smith glanced up and then tossed the knife he'd been working on into a wooden box. Sweat glistened on his shirtless back and metal dust had stained his fingers the oily gray of storm clouds. Similar smudges on his chest and face made him appear as if he'd painted himself for a battle.

Beatrice hung at a distance while Kerel showed him the locket. The smith pinched the face piece between his fingers and studied it. He motioned Beatrice to come closer. "What do you know about this, *cher*?"

She stepped up behind Kerel to look at the jewel lying on the smith's rough palm. The grackle clucked and fluttered anxiously in his cage. "Mamzelle Rosabel gave it to Tante Abeille and Tante Abeille left it for me." She pointed to the scripted word that began with an *R*. "That says Rosabel, doesn't it?"

The smith rubbed some of the black from his fingers into the grooves of the etched words so that they were easier to see against the shiny silver. He lowered his voice. "You know letters? The old man teaching you?"

She shook her head. "I hold the books when he reads aloud. I've learned a little bit that way, but not enough to read on my own."

"A priest in Ayti taught me. He was curious to know if a slave could be taught to read Scripture. I surprised him." The smith gestured at Kerel. "As you already know, the boy is learning; I could teach you too."

Kerel groaned in disbelief. He started to make protest, but the smith quieted him with a stern look. "I teach him in the early morning if you want to join us," he offered. "This in exchange for keeping our secret, of course."

"Thank you, but I can't leave the maison until Michie takes his nap after lunch," Beatrice said. Kerel's obvious relief annoyed her. "Can you tell me the words in my locket before I leave, Monsieur Gú?"

"I'll fix it for you, but I'll not tell what's scripted

in it. To know that you'll learn to read on your own, or you'll ask the old man to read for you." He closed his fist around the jewel and jangled it. "Your choice, but I can tell you Reynard has reason not to tell you the truth and he'd probably take it from you." He opened his hand and held the locket out for Beatrice. When she didn't reach for it he smiled and folded it inside his cast-off shirt. "You understand then? Your ignorance gives him power over you."

He bent and took a knife from the pile to be sharpened, held it up to his eye to consider the blade's edge. "I can't stop work in midday to teach you—not so near harvest with the mules needing shoes, and the cane wagons to fix, and the kettles in the sugarhouse still to be mended. Kerel is ahead of you in learning. If you'll come he can teach you in the afternoons."

Kerel and Beatrice both made choking, sputtering noises. But the smith deftly stroked the blade over the sharpening stone and pretended not to hear.

* * *

Neither she nor Kerel felt comfortable with the arrangement. And they knew her going to the smith shop every day would kindle suspicion. Since he couldn't very well visit her at the maison, or any of the buildings where others might see them, they agreed to meet on some days in a secret place Kerel had made for himself away from the quarter.

It was a small cleared space in a cane field. The entrance to it from the rutted wagon path was marked only by a slight parting in the cane stalks, and easily missed. Kerel lead her to it once, and then every time after waited for her there.

The space was roomlike and shaped like an egg. The floor was carpeted with a layer of dry cane leaves, and the ceiling was of rippling live leaves that looked like ranks of green rooster's tails. Any noise they made by talking was masked by the racket of the cicadas and muffled by the cane. At the smith's shop Kerel practiced writing on a slate with a stick of charcoal, but in the cane he taught her letters by scratching them in the earth. They reminded

Beatrice of the *vevers*—the name symbols—that Tante Abeille had drawn on the floor with flour and wood ash to summon *loa* spirits to ceremonies. *Loa* came to their *vever* because they could not resist seeing their own name revealed to the world.

Beatrice collected scraps of paper from the trash and took a half-empty pot of ink from Michie's desk. When Tante Perte roasted a brown turkey, Beatrice asked Zina for the tail feathers. The shafts, notched at a slant, held ink, and she practiced writing letters at night when there was moonlight to see by. She tried stringing letters together that she thought belonged in her name. Over and over she wrote *B-E-A-T-R-I-S*, relying on the sounds of the letters, loving the way the ink swirled across the page in loops and lines. She understood how the *loa* felt about the *vevers.* There was magic in seeing your name.

Without Kerel, and the smith, she wouldn't have known it.

She took a book from the study, the smallest one she could find, slim enough that the gap it left was easily filled by rearranging the surrounding volumes. Michie had a hundred books, or more. One book didn't matter to him.

She hid it beneath her skirts before she met Kerel in the cane. "Turn around and close your eyes," she told him. He did so, but mumbling that he'd already seen her underskirt once if that's what she was worried about.

When she let him open his eyes and see the surprise, he shoved the book away like it might bite him. "Take it back!" he hissed.

"Why? Michie's got shelves and shelves. He won't know it's gone." She saw he wanted it, and pressed it into his hands. Reluctantly he took it and thumbed through the pages, some of which had pictures of plants and animals engraved on them. He closed it carefully and laid it aside. "I have something for you too," he said. He pulled a cloth from his pocket and unwrapped the locket. "There's a new pin in the hinge and the catch is tightened."

Beatrice opened the case and rubbed her fingertip over the darkened script inside it. The fancy curling letters scarcely looked like those Kerel was teaching her; in fact they looked more like the twining wisteria vines outside her window than words.

She asked him to clasp the chain at the back of her neck. His breath was warm and close, and he smelled of metal and smoke; his fingertips brushed her skin in a shivery way that made her breath catch. Rather than draw letters in the dirt, they spent the rest of their time with heads together over the open book.

Beatrice didn't tend well to Michie the rest of that day. Her mind wandered too often, and she was slow coming to him when he rang his bell. He read aloud, but her thoughts were on Kerel. Finally, after Michie barked at her in frustration and called her scatterbrained, she told him she felt ill, and he let her go to her room early.

She did not rest, but sat at the open window and watched the river change color from steel gray to dusk-blushed pink, brought to life by the setting sun.

CHAPTER TWELVE

Dreams

"**D**REAMS are a true sign of life," the smith said, tapping the scar on his forehead. "A person who sleeps and doesn't dream is already dead. I heard it called *dromi l'mort*—sleep of the dead."

Beatrice was waiting for Kerel to fetch the slate and had asked the smith what he thought it meant to sleep without dreams. She'd pretended it was Michie's problem, rather than her own. But that she woke every morning without memory of any dream seemed odd and bothered her. *Dromi l'mort* was a good name for such empty, quiet slumber. She wondered if the feather mattress was the cause. Maybe it was too soft and inspired too deep a sleep.

Her visions had also stopped; at first a relief but now a source of longing. She'd had none since Tante Abeille ran away from the plantation, not a one since she'd moved into the maison with Michie. He exhausted her patience. Scarcely allowed her out of his sight anymore, not even to visit with Tante Perte and Tante Las in the cookhouse. Her teeth clenched at the sound of his infernal bell chiming. Her world inside the maison was much smaller than it had ever been when she'd lived in the quarter. She missed the company of other women, the chatter and warmth of the kitchen, and her work there and in the garden.

Tante Abeille had been right about the garden failing when she was gone—though it hadn't failed so much as reinvented itself. Untended and unchecked, it did whatever it pleased. The roots of noble old flowers now mingled beneath the soil with those of humble oxeye daisies and brown-eyed Susans, butterfly weed, and bee balm. The bees seemed to prefer the hardy commoners that threatened to soon overwhelm the more delicate and needful plants she and Tante had pampered for so long.

The rambling briar was laden with wine-dark autumn fruit. Birds feasted, greedy and mindless of the thorny canes. Wasps and bees claimed the over-ripe berries that dropped to the ground. After sipping their fill of fermented juice, they flew in drunken swoops through the air, or lazed in the sun daydreaming. Zina picked basins full of fruit for Tante Perte to use in sweet pastries, or to mix with sugar to make jam.

Beatrice wasn't sure if Zina knew she was meeting Kerel in secret, or if she pitied Beatrice for the cramped life she now had, but her scowls and glares had finally softened. Sometimes she stopped outside the back door to speak a word or two to Beatrice. At least until the honeybees on the briar caught wind of them and began to collect on Beatrice's skirts in great enough numbers to send Zina running.

The smith had returned to the work of repairing a wagon wheel's metal rim when Kerel joined Beatrice in a hidden nook at the back of the shop for their lesson. Their time was hurried now as harvest approached, and they met more at the shop rather than in the cane field. He'd put on a shirt that was mostly ribbons of cloth loosely held together by seams. His arms and chest and face were flecked with new pink burns that made him look as if he'd been christened with sparks of fire rather than with drops of holy water. Rather than thinking him ugly, she found the scars made him as interesting to look at as a sky at night when patterns in the stars could be imagined, and wishes cast. She resisted the urge to tell him or to reach out and trace them with her fingertip.

Heavy clusters of wisteria blooms hung like grapes at the sides of the bedroom window. Beatrice curled on the floor beneath it and watched gauzy clouds drift veil-like across Mawu's full, silver face. On such a night Tante Abeille would have lit an oil lamp and drawn a *vever* and shook the *asson* to call the ancestor spirits. She'd said it was sacred and full of power, and she'd treasured it.

That's why Beatrice couldn't understand what had made Tante abandon it in the pasture where it was sure to be ruined or lost. Luckily the overseer had found it and brought it to Michie. But then he'd put it in the trash bin. By luck Zina had retrieved it and traded it to Beatrice for a hand mirror and a comb. It was a miracle that the *asson* had found its way into her hands.

Beatrice rolled to her belly and retrieved it from beneath her bed. She shook it gently, listening to the snake bones tumble inside it and watched the moonlight play off the colored beads that were strung over it. The sound it made was a soothing *shhh-shhh-shhhh*—the noise Zina made to calm little Frey. Shaken louder, it became the sound of wind-shivered cane around her and Kerel in the field. Louder still, it was as vibrant as the call of the cicadas at dusk. She wondered if the *loa* listened to the *asson* because it reminded them of the living world, and woke them from their *dromi l'mort*.

Whether it was that the turn of the season had cooled the evening air, or that she slept on the floor, Beatrice dreamed vividly. Not an unpleasant dream, but a disturbing one: a woman stood on the far bank of a gray misty river. She held a glowing pearl of light in her hand, and though she whispered, her voice spanned the water. She had a voice similar to Tante Abeille's—the same quiet authority and crackling dryness—but she wasn't Tante.

Find me, she called. *I am waiting.*

At the sound of his own voice, Reynard woke with a start. His heart galloped against his breastbone. And his cheeks felt sticky. They were glazed with half-dried tears and he scrubbed at them with the back of his hand—a claw he scarcely recognized anymore as his hand: brown-spotted and ropy, his nails thick and yellowed as horn. He could barely butter his own bread, or put spoon to mouth without spilling down his shirtfront. He cursed his hands for their tremors and curled his twitching fingers into fists. His frailty enraged him. And frightened him.

Or maybe the nightmare he'd woken from was still bright in his mind. Especially the dry rattling of insects; a plague of them on the wing, so dense they cloaked the sun. Derora had called to him through the shivering noise: *Come to me. I am waiting for you.*

He would have in an instant, but she was far away, separated from him by a vast field of sugarcane. And he'd had no cane knife to clear a path, and no field hand to wield it for him.

Derora was dead and buried in some secret place. But he believed in spirits, and if ever a spirit could speak, it would be hers. She'd had uncanny powers—dreams and visions of the future. His life had been saved by a vision, and his fortune made by another. Yet he'd sent Derora away before she gave birth to Ara—and she had died for it while the squalling brat had lived. It was a bad dream of the persistent sort, one that always lingered at the edges of memory and visited too often.

It began on the day Derora had begged him not to travel to N'Orléans. "The river will swallow you and your boat," she'd warned, tearful. "Stay here with me."

Her worrying flattered him, but he chided her for it and told her he would be fine. She cried and carried on so till he gave in and sent the boat ahead, promising to follow by horse. Next morning the news reached him that the boiler on the barge had exploded and a fire had consumed the boat. All aboard died horribly.

His first thought had been that Derora had knowledge of a plot against him, but when he questioned her, she told a far-fetched story about an old power given to her people in an ancient time by a pagan goddess of the moon. "I am a seer," she said. "It's my gift to see what can't be seen."

Slaves were known to be superstitious, believers in witches and fortune-tellers. "Ah, but you saw the river swallow me, and here I stand!" he said. "Your vision was false, *cher.*"

"What is seen can be changed in small ways, sometimes. The boat sank as I saw it—that couldn't be changed. But I kept you safe here with me." Her voice had the patient tone of a tutor speaking to a slow pupil, and it irritated him. He was not her student, but her master.

"Prove it again," he had demanded. "Tell me another thing that will happen. How far will your sight reach?"

She drew back and let his hands go. Then she took a deep breath and turned to stare out of the window beyond his shoulder. He waited quietly, bothered by how few times she blinked. Her eyes ticked back and forth in their sockets until finally her lids fluttered and she gasped as if she'd been holding her breath. She winced and pushed her palms against her brows. "There will be an early freeze, Reynard. Bring your cane in early or it will all go to ruin."

He had doubted her and waited, knowing an early freeze could turn whole fields of ripe cane to worthless mush in a single night. Men didn't make business decisions based on female hunches, or hoodoo beliefs. They consulted the almanac and charted the weather, and made predictions based on practical measurements. Still, her certainty needled him.

"How can you be sure it will freeze early?" he had asked over and over. "Tell me the exact date."

She was certain, but the day she couldn't name, only that it would be. He must trust her, and believe.

Finally, reluctantly, feeling very foolish, he gave the order to have the cane harvested early. It took the better part of two weeks to bring most of it in and fill the boilers of his sugarhouse with pressed juice. He had a small strip of one field left to cut on the night the freeze swept over Louisián. Overnight, nearly all the cane in the parish froze and withered. He earned a fortune at market, while his neighbors' fortunes rotted in their fields. Out of desperation they sold arpent after arpent of those fields, and he watched the boundaries of his land grow wider.

Later, in a shop in Orléans he had spent a few coins on a silver trinket, a small token to make Derora content with him. Neither of them knew it yet, but the early frost had spoiled more than the cane. Forever afterward he loved the seer and the fortune she could give him more than he loved the woman.

"What do you see when you search for the two of us together?" he had asked her, teasing, confident.

"Spring doesn't worry itself over winter," she answered with happiness that sounded false. "Let's enjoy these days without thought of others."

He thought her very wise.

Then one day toward the end of summer she announced, "I carry your child."

Immediately he felt ice collect behind his breastbone and chill his heart. Bile rose in his throat at the shame a child would bring him.

Such things were not uncommon, and barely scandalous among the cane planters of Louisián. It was his mother, Madame Rillieux, that he feared. Though she preferred to live abroad in France and let him run the plantation, the property was hers by title until she died. If she discovered, through some acquaintance, that he had tainted Grandpère's noble blood by having a child with a slave, she'd punish him. Madame was proud and vindictive, and she'd not hesitate to strip him of everything.

"I won't claim it!" he snapped at Derora.

More cruel words leaped out hot and fast, too terrible to remember, but they wiped the smile from Derora's face more completely than if he'd slapped her.

He'd sent her to live again in the quarter with Abeille until the baby's birth.

Abeille had brought the newborn to him, holding the tender bundle in her rough crow's claws. "It's a girl-baby. She's like coffee and cream, with light-colored eyes, too." Her voice croaked with accusation. Her eyes struck at him as hard as a hammer on an anvil.

"All newborns are light," he told her without looking at the baby, without interest. "Has she named the father?"

Abeille stiffened her spine and pulled the child back toward her protectively. "*Non*, she didn't. I come here with the child to show she is healthy. My sister asks for nothing but that her daughter's name be marked in your book as Ara."

He stared at the woman furiously, and she at him, until his eyes watered with the effort and he blinked. With the painted Rosabel as silent witness, he wrote the baby's name in his ledger. A small price to pay.

"Keep the brat with you and raise her," he said to Abeille. "When Derora is well enough, send her back to me."

"Your heart is mastered by greed," Abeille hissed.

"I am mastered by nothing!" he bellowed, and would have struck her down had she not been holding the baby.

Four days later the overseer brought word that Derora had died of birth fever. It still grieved him to remember. Though many years had passed, it brought nightmares.

I am mastered by nothing, he repeated, and laughed silently, wretchedly at his own arrogance.

Age had mastered him. And loneliness. And regret.

Old Abeille no longer slept or dreamed. At night she rested with her sisters and waited for the yolky-tasting sunlight to warm the hive and get them all moving again. During the day she worked as she always had in the garden, though no one took notice of her. She liked what the garden had become: unkempt and blousy, spilling over with field flowers whose seeds had drifted down and taken root hither and yon. She preferred the bolder reds and yellows and oranges of their blooms better than the milky pinks and creams of the fussier flowers that always wilted by afternoon. She enjoyed the surprising smell and taste of candyweed, butterweed, sweet pea, and morning glory.

Nectar, pollen, light, heat—these were her main concerns. Little else mattered or interested her until she heard the *asson*. The sound plucked at her, conjured memory, pulled her back to who she'd been: daughter of Mawu, sister of Derora, tante to Ara and Beatrice.

Abeille quivered. Those resting close against her felt her excitement. She had no need of words in order to speak with them or make them understand. Dance was their language, and it told a story quite well indeed.

Though Abeille was new among them, and her movements had a foreign flair, they recognized the steps to a favorite old nursery tale. Everyone knew the story about a colony of honeybees that escaped one by one from the hives of a greedy beekeeper, but Abeille's version was stirring and powerful, urgent and beautiful.

When she finished, they buzzed approvingly. None had ever slept, or had a true dream, but it seemed a story told as well as that must be very close to dreaming—a lovely shared dream.

CHAPTER THIRTEEN

Harvest

THE AIR in autumn hummed with energy and had an odor that came only with sugar harvest. The cane fields smelled most complex— the nutty greenness of oozing cane sap mingling with the musky scent of human sweat as the fields fell in waves before the cane cutters. Beatrice woke each morning to the sound of their songs and their blades thwacking through the crisp stalks.

By middle-day the overpowering smell of

burned caramel mingled with that of sap and sweat. Smoke from burning heaps of cane leaves and pressed cane pulp smudged out the sun, and flakes of ash fell like soft black snow. Syrup bubbled in copper boilers inside the sugarhouse where wasps were a menace, lured in droves by the soured pulp piles outside and the sticky film of sugar that coated walls and floor inside.

For the first time in memory Beatrice did not help with the harvest or the making of sugar. In fact she had no work but to fetch for Michie, or fan him, or sit idly at the upstairs window and watch barges laden with sugar slide downriver like sand through an hourglass. She'd become a house pet, like the primped little dog that belonged to the old spinster lady Beatrice called "Madame tutor." Madame came three days a week to instruct her in dance and demeanor, in preparation for the grand fête to be held at the maison following the sugar harvest.

When Beatrice learned too slowly or complained, Madame ranted, "How can I be expected to turn a sow's ear into a silk purse? I am not a magician!" Or she'd rap Beatrice's ankles with her baton and warn, "You'll not be ready for the fête, and Monsieur will do worse than rap your feet!"

The fête was to be in three days' time, but Beatrice knew she'd be ready. A dressmaker from Orléans had sewn her a green silk dress in a style current in Paris. She'd learned to sit and walk properly in the stiff whalebone corset. And she'd talked Kerel into practicing the dance steps with her in their cane hollow. It made her happy beyond words to feel the moist heat from his palm on her waist and his callused fingers gently twined with hers. To be so close embarrassed him and made him clumsy, which always made her laugh.

Beatrice closed her eyes and swayed silently. She wanted to dance again with Kerel and laugh. Like the silver locket, she felt as though some missing part of her had been found at last. He was more than her milk-twin. He was her soul-twin—*marasa* by choice rather than birth.

She'd been as restless and irritable as Kerel's caged grackle. The last time she'd seen his bird, it had lifted up on its feet and beat its wing tips desperately against the bars of the cage. That's exactly how she felt inside the maison, wretchedly listening to the hall clock count all the moments since she'd last seen Kerel.

Finally, she stole downstairs and pressed her cheek to the library door. She listened for a while to the overseer and Michie discuss the price of sugar and the need for more field hands. It being week's end, she knew the overseer's report would be longer than usual and give her enough time to escape the house. As she slipped past the garden, a party of honeybees gathered and trailed behind her as she made her way through the quarter.

Kerel stood with his arms around the neck of one of the mules that turned the press wheel. He stroked its face, his scarred cheek resting against the beast's long bony jaw. And Beatrice saw that he crooned soft words to it, and that the mule seemed perfectly entranced with whatever he said, for it scarcely moved a muscle. A good thing, considering the smith held the animal's rear foot between his knees, measuring the arch of the hoof for a new shoe. As Beatrice drew near, the mule's ear swiveled toward her, but it made no other sign to acknowledge her, and neither did Kerel or the blacksmith until the hoof rested securely on the ground.

"Aren't you worried it will kick?" she asked, and the smith shook his head. "Kerel has a way with beasts, true. They listen to him. I've seen him call squirrels off the branch to eat from his hand. Birds, too. I didn't know better, I'd say he's gifted with beast-speak."

Kerel shrugged his shoulders and yawned enormously.

The grackle's cage hung in a shady eave, and the bird leaped from one side to the other in stunted flight. Kerel clucked at it, and it cocked its head and answered him with a *jeeb-jeeb*. Beatrice looked

into one of its bright yellow eyes and felt a wash of
kinship. How could he have a way with animals and
not see that the bird was miserable?

"You should let it go," Beatrice said.

Kerel had no brows to lift, but his forehead
rose slightly. "I raised it from a hatchling. Outside
the cage it wouldn't survive. Might not even know
how to use its wings."

The smith grunted and shook his head, but
offered no comment.

"If it were mine I'd give it a chance."

"But it's not yours," Kerel snapped, and then
softened his tone. "You have everything you want,
living like a fine lady in the maison. I have a bird.
If I let it go, I have nothing anymore that's mine."

I'm yours, Beatrice thought to say, but didn't.
Allowing herself such a bold thought tied her
tongue in knots. In truth, she and Kerel belonged
to Michie, and no one in the quarter could court
or marry without permission from him. Her feelings
for Kerel were best left unspoken and protected.

It grew late in the day, nearly sunset, but the cicadas rattled on at full pitch, filling the silence that fell over the shop. The cane cutters sang with weary voices in the distance, keeping to the rhythm of their blades. Arpent after arpent of ripened cane fell, expanding the horizon and revealing the hidden warrens of rabbits, the dens of mice, the covens of quail.

The secret hollow in the cane where she and Kerel usually met was probably gone, Beatrice realized; every one of the sheltering stalks cut to the ground and sent to the mill. She wanted Kerel to walk there with her, but didn't ask. He and the smith were still busy at their work, but before she left them at it she asked Kerel to practice steps with her one more time.

"A lady waits for a beaux to ask her to dance, not the other way," he grumbled. Color rose to his cheeks, darkening the scars.

"Then a lady might wait forever to dance," she countered, swishing her skirts in mock irritation.

The smith laughed and gave Kerel a push

toward her. "When a lady asks for a dance, you must count your luck and leap to your feet. If I had two good ones I'd show you how it's done in Ayti! I'd dance a circle round you both."

"Someone might see us," Kerel said, worried.

The smith gestured toward a back corner partially shielded from view by shadows and a stacked collection of ironwork railing. "I'll keep watch. You dance while you have the chance."

Sighing heavily, Kerel bowed and extended his hand to Beatrice in the way Madame tutor had told her a gentleman would at a fête. She curtsied slightly and laid her fingers lightly atop his palm, and let him lead her to the back of the smith shop. Dusty light filtered through the gaps where the roof met the brick wall and forge chimney. Glittering specks swirled about them as Kerel rested his hand on her waist and she gathered her skirts to keep from tripping over them. With their other hands twined they moved slowly in the boxy pattern Madame tutor called "waltz." Madame had taught Beatrice the complicated steps of the quadrille, too, but Bea had only shown Kerel the waltz. Partners changed in the quadrille; they let go and moved apart. In the waltz, partners stayed together, touching until song's end.

Maybe because the space was small, Kerel pulled Beatrice closer than what Madame would call proper. She could smell him—smoke and metal. His right leg bumped against hers through her skirt. They moved smoothly, without speaking, listening to the rhythmic scuff of their feet and the matched in-and-out of their breathing. The box pattern grew smaller until they were only swaying back and forth. Beatrice tilted her face to better see Kerel's eyes, and at that movment he bent to her and smothered her mouth with his.

"Someone's coming!" the smith called and they pulled away as the grackle began to clatter a warning.

Zina rushed toward them. "Have you seen Frey?" she asked, nearly in tears. "I looked up and he was gone from the kitchen! None of us noticed him leaving. Las thought he might've come to see you, Kerel."

"He's not here," Beatrice told her. Kerel shook his head in agreement. Zina covered her mouth with her hands and began to sob. "It's late, he'll be scared in the dark. . . ."

Beatrice wondered if finding a boy was much like finding a needle. She sank to the ground and focused her mind on Frey's face. She heard him first, humming a childish tune, and turned her mind's eye toward the sound, then followed it through a dark tunnel until she caught sight of him. Frey held a stone the size of an apple in his hand. With great effort he cocked his arm and heaved it away, nearly toppling over. Beatrice couldn't follow the stone's path; it was all she could do to hold the boy in her mind, and she didn't dare take her eye from him.

Less than a moment after the rock left Frey's hand, she heard a splash, as if a frog had jumped into the shallows of a pond. The boy clapped and squealed with delight, then humming again, squatted down to find another stone.

Beatrice opened her eyes. Zina still had her hands over her face. Hardly a second had passed. "Frey is somewhere near water, Zina. Kerel and the smith can check the riverbank. You go to the old well behind the maison. There's a pond between the pasture and the cane fields—I'll check there."

Beatrice took the cart path through the shorn cane, moving as quickly as she dared without falling or twisting her ankle in the deep ruts. She barely noticed the sound of hoofs hitting the dirt path behind her. A jaybird cried out a warning from the cane, and before she could leap away into the field, the overseer danced his horse beside her and caught her beneath one arm. With a quick jerk, he dragged her up and clamped a hand around her waist, pressing her close against him.

"Old man's been calling for you, pet," he rasped in her ear, "wondering where it was you went off to. I told him I'd know where to find you. What goes on in the quarter t'aint a secret from me. I know about what you been up to with the smith's boy out in these cane fields."

Beatrice's mouth went dry and her stomach roiled queasily beneath the overseer's gloved hand. He whistled between his teeth and then clucked his tongue. "You both in deep trouble."

But for a single beeswax candle burning uneasily inside a glass shade on the desk, the library was unnaturally dark for the hour. Michie sat in one of the chairs beside the fireless hearth, deathly still except for his hands, which always twitched of their own accord in his lap. He did not turn when the overseer pushed Beatrice into the room, nor did he bother to look up at her, or speak when she stood directly before him.

The overseer cleared his throat and said, "She was out in the fields. Likely on her way to meet up with the boy I told you about."

Michie Reynard looked pale as the candle that flickered nearby. "Take her upstairs and lock her in her room," he croaked. "Bring the smith and the boy to me."

Upstairs, Beatrice raced to the half-open window and waited to catch sight of Kerel and the smith. As the overseer led them past the garden toward the back door she resisted the impulse to call out a warning—to scream, "Run!" But calling out would only make things worse, and there was nowhere to run. So Beatrice watched them in frightened silence as they entered the maison.

After a time she heard the turning of a key in the lock and the sound of dishes clattering. As soon as Zina entered the room with a tray, the door was shut behind her and locked again from outside. Her face was pinched and grim, and she set the tray down with force enough to slosh most of the water out of the pitcher. "How did you know Frey was at the river?"

"I saw him there," Beatrice answered. Zina

crossed herself and mopped at the spill on the table.

"Tell me what's happening to Kerel," Beatrice said. "Have they found out about the reading?"

"Can't you close your eyes and see? It's not about reading; it's worse than that. Overseer told Michie that Kerel lures you to meet with him in secret, and that his intentions toward you aren't innocent."

"A lie!"

Zina narrowed her eyes. "Lie or not, Kerel will be lashed, and come harvest end they plan to send him away with a man invited to the fête—some cotton lord lives in the east." She knocked on the door and waited for it to be opened. As she crossed the threshold she turned and said, "They say devil gives and takes with the same hand. I thank you for finding my son today but you've cost me my own brother in the same turn." With one hand she made the gesture against evil—a thing she'd not done for a long time—and then with the other hand touched her fingers to her heart and her mouth and sent a kiss toward Beatrice.

Beatrice kneeled at the window, nervously snapping the locket open and closed. Below her the overseer pushed Kerel through the back door so that he stumbled down the steps and sprawled belly-down on the brick path. When Kerel tried to rise, the overseer pushed his foot into the small of his back, then leaned down and ripped his tattered shirt from tail to neck. With the smith standing near and Beatrice watching, he delivered twenty stinging blows across Kerel's shoulders with his riding crop, and then two more across one cheek, bloodying the corner of the boy's mouth.

Kerel didn't move until the overseer was gone. The smith reached down to gather him up in his powerful arms and carried him inside the kitchen.

Beatrice realized she'd covered her mouth with both hands to keep from screaming. Screaming would have made the beating worse. Already this was her fault. Zina was right; everyone was right. She was cursed like Maman and Abeille—bad luck.

She lifted the locket from around her neck and held it close to her eyes. Only a thin wash of gray light remained of the day, and she used it to study the relief of vines and flowers that twined over the jewel: a miniature garden captured in metal the color of moonlight, guarded by a silver bee.

Maybe it truly was a charm or talisman, long broken until she found the missing half in the garden. The smith had joined the halves together for her, and he and Kerel together had given her the key to decipher what was hidden inside. Maybe it was an incantation to break the curse and set her free. Like Kerel's grackle, it was all she had.

She unhooked the bee clasp so that it released the tiny silver bud. The two halves of the locket swung apart like the unlatched door of the grackle's cage. Beatrice brought the locket close to her eyes and studied the etched script, blackened still with soot from the smith's fingers. The letters were different from the blocky ones she knew how to read. These were curled and linked together like tendrils. With her elbows resting on the window's ledge so that she could catch the last of the day's light and the first of the moonlight, she began the difficult work of guessing the letters and stringing together their sounds until they made sense.

From the kitchen window the smith watched her. She seemed to be in prayer.

CHAPTER FOURTEEN

Grackle

EATRICE strained forward so that the moonlight pooled in her hands and glinted on the locket. Her knees hurt from kneeling; her eyes and head hurt from the strain of reading in poor light; and her heart ached at what words she'd pieced together inside the charm. She closed her hands around it and felt the silver bee clasp the little silver bud with a gentle click, once again hiding the words away. When she opened her hands the locket lay there like a fat drop of Mawu's light made solid as quicksilver.

The full meaning of what she'd read settled over her heavy as the stone wheel that crushed the cane. It said, *For my Derora, With love, Reynard.* The locket had never belonged to Mamzelle Rosabel, but to Grandmère.

Beatrice scrambled across the floor and pounded her fists on the door. She screamed until her throat felt raw, and finally, from the bottom of the stairs, she heard Michie bellow for her to stop. His slow footsteps treaded the stairs and then over the floor in the hall. He hesitated outside her door, saying nothing, but she heard the labor in his breathing. She pounded the door in the spot where she imagined his face to be.

"That boy isn't worth all of this," he barked. "He isn't good enough."

"Why not? I belong in the quarter, not locked away in this room."

"Not true. You belong here with me."

"Not true!" she countered, silently adding, *and neither did Grandmère!*

Reynard said nothing, but she could feel his fury through the wood. As his footsteps moved away, Beatrice threw herself across the rug and lay weeping until she retched and no more tears would come. All about her, pretty things glinted and sparkled in the moon glow. The rug felt warm against her feet. The bed invited her, soft and deep.

"Let me go!" she yelled for the thousandth time. She emptied every drawer, tipped tables, tore linens, ripped, wrecked, and smashed everything. Slopped wash-water atop the feather bed; soiled the rug with fireplace ash. She left nothing whole or untouched by her bitterness. It drove her. She tasted it, green pecan hulls and vinegar mixed and put to boil.

A dark clot gathered on the sill of the open window, at first no larger than a spattered lump of wet cinders, but the stain spread quickly, its fingers lengthening until it reached across wall and ceiling.

And as it grew, so did a vibrant humming that charged the air with such urgency that it summoned Beatrice to pay attention. It drew her toward the window and the shadowed wall—not shadowed but as though covered with rippling velvet: the bodies of living bees that had taken the shape of a woman. Tante Abeille spoke from the midst of them. "I see you've wasted time causing room—rain—ruin!"

Perhaps, wherever she was, she'd forgotten the meanings of words. Beatrice crawled toward the voice. "Tante! You've come back for me!"

"I was here, *piti*. Wanting—wasting—waiting for you to come to yourself."

"Are you a spirit now? A *loa*? Can you use your power to help me?"

The body of honeybees buzzed more shrilly. "*Non!* You are your own hop—hope—help! If you think the room is a trap, then it is. You believe four walls can hold you, and so they do. I'm no *loa*. I am old and tired and nearly spent with waiting and hoping. What power is left to me I'll use to protect you, but you must find the way out. Find your own true power, not just needles and buttons, but who you were meant to bee—be—Bea.

"Cast a stone—look far and truly see. Use the *asson*, but only do what little you must. There is always a prince—prize—price. . . ."

The dark, pulsing stain on the wall shrank as the bees poured over the windowsill into the dark garden. A breeze stirred the heavy air inside the bedroom. The lace curtains fluttered and then snapped back sharply as the breeze grew stronger. Below the window the bees spun wildly until they became a whirling windstorm that lifted into the night sky and then scattered apart like the blown seeds of a dandelion.

Many of the bees had lingered too long and had been left behind in the room. They buzzed about in agitated and aimless paths. Some lit on Beatrice; she felt them land gently in her hair and on her shoulders. They brushed feelers over her skin, unrolled their tongues and licked her, gave her bee kisses. She let them, unable to bring herself to move or care. Tante Abeille had abandoned her once again. Maybe forever.

The night and following day passed slowly. Beatrice did not eat or drink what Zina brought to her, nor did she speak. She sat by the window and held the silver locket in one hand and the *asson* in the other while Zina fussed about trying to straighten the ruined bedroom. When Beatrice refused to help her with it, she stopped, saying, "Then you'll have to live in this mess or fix it yourself."

By evening Beatrice felt lightheaded but still refused to allow food or water to pass her lips. Empty as a gourd, her mind adrift, she'd begun to hear the voice she'd almost forgotten calling, *"I'm waiting. Find me."* She could almost reach out and touch the spirit across the dark water. She understood the water would take her to the spirit and save her.

Exasperated with Beatrice, Zina threatened to alert Michie, but instead returned with Tante Las in tow. Tante settled herself on a stool in front of Beatrice. "You mustn't make yourself sick like this," she said. "The fête is tomorrow and Michie will be more than angry if you can't attend. You're the reason for it."

Beatrice slid her hand into Tante Las's but remained silent until the two women left her to return to the work of readying the maison for the morrow's celebration.

Mawu shone down on dark fields that bled into dark sky so that neither was separate from the other. A few fireflies blinked in the garden like small, dry sparks, and the humble cricket song lifted up from the hedgerows and weedy places as the cicadas quieted in the trees and canebrakes.

From beyond the kitchen a grackle winged its way toward the window where Beatrice sat. It landed on the wisteria vine and cocked its head so that one yellow eye caught hers. In a blink it leaped away and disappeared into the dusk, then wheeled back and landed this time in the bramble below her.

Tante Abeille's words ran through her mind in an unending circle. *"Look far. Truly see. Cast another stone. Use the* asson.*"*

She had always known her talent for finding little things lost. The locket she had found by accident or luck, just like anyone who had no talent for finding found such things. She knew where to find little Frey because she had thought of him and gone where that thought led her, where she knew he would be. But what had happened with the smith and her visions in the garden were more than finding: they were about seeing. She controlled finding, while seeing took control of her: the first a talent, the second a curse. Yet they seemed two sides of one coin. To find a thing, she first had to imagine it, she had to see it—if only in her mind's eye.

Dizzy with hunger and lack of sleep, Beatrice closed her eyes and shook the *asson.* The air tasted of the harvest, smoke and sugar, but she filled her lungs deeply and worked to slow her racing heart. She'd never tried to work a spell, never wanted the talent to be hers. Until now.

"Come *loa*, come *mort*," she whispered, remembering Tante Abeille's prayers and shaking the *asson*. "Hear me call to you. My eyes are open. Show me what I should and must see."

Without thought or direction, she waited— her mind an empty gourd to be filled—with what she didn't know. Perhaps a sign, or a word, or a picture, or an urge.

The night seemed to hold its breath for a while, and then one cricket and another chirruped from outside. And the tree frogs trilled. The bees in the room joined them, though their song was less joyful. A rain owl called out mournfully from the alley of live oaks. *Hoo, hoo, ooo-hooo . . .*

Beatrice felt her mind flicker and stray from its task of empty waiting. She thought of Grandmère Derora, and this time her mind moved in a swift and certain path, much as it did when she searched for a needle or coin. But it felt more like memory in the way her thoughts reeled backward, like Michie flipping the pages of one of his books until the correct page fell open.

She found herself in Tante Abeille's cabin. She had the sensation of hanging batlike from the rafters while peering down at two women: a younger Abeille and another woman who took a cup from Abeille's hand, saying, "I won't really die if I drink it?"

"*Non*, Derora," Abeille answered. "It's potent, but you'll only seem dead. Breath so faint it'll not even mist a mirror. I'll say you died of birth fever. When the time comes I have another potion to wake you."

"Promise you won't let them bury me! And you'll take care of Ara until she comes of age?"

"*Oui, cher*. It's the least I can do to fix what my hand started. I've paid dearly for that charm."

Derora laid her cheek on Abeille's arm. "You were tricked."

"Now another trick," Abeille said, "and once it's done, I will come to you with Ara as soon as I can. As soon as she's old enough to find you with her sight. You mustn't send word. Trust no one."

Derora kissed the infant laying beside her on the bed and drained the cup. "Find me, daughter," she said. "I'll be waiting for you." In a moment she collapsed. Abeille cried out, then held a palm over her sister's face to check for breath. Trembling, she pressed closed each eyelid as she would have a corpse.

Beatrice watched as Derora was carried to the maison and prepared for burial. She saw a dark-haired Michie weep over her in a silk-lined casket. And Beatrice hovered nearby as Abeille stole into the parlor during the night, just before dawn.

She took a vial from her waist pouch and pried open her sister's mouth with her fingers. She unstoppered the little bottle and dribbled a tonic onto Derora's tongue. As quickly as she'd collapsed, Derora opened her eyes and took a deep shuddering breath. Shakily she crawled from the casket into Abeille's arms, leaving her *tignon* behind on the silk pillow. Derora stopped on the garden path and removed the locket from her neck. She opened it, twisted it apart at the hinges, and flung it into the garden. Moonlit, the silver chain and the half-locket it carried resembled a shooting star, its arcing path easily traced to the mossy edge of the garden path. The second half of the locket disappeared in the dark, lost in the litter beneath the white rose.

The two women climbed the levee and ran upriver until they reached a thicket where a little rowboat waited with the smith at the oars. Then the vision faltered, but through the gathering haze Beatrice heard Derora call out, "I'll be waiting!"

Beatrice woke at first light. She'd slept leaning against the wall beneath the window and felt moist with dew, as if she'd slept in the garden under the rose again. She got to her knees and peered out of the window at it. She heard a grackle call *jeeb-jeeb* before she spotted it, still perched within the bramble, mindless of the honeybees darting about. It saw her and quickly flew up to the wisteria vine, ruffled its neck feathers, and then swooped away over the kitchen roof toward the smith shop. Beatrice wondered if it was Kerel's bird.

When Zina entered the room with a breakfast tray, Beatrice said, "A grackle came to my window last night and again this morning. Is it Kerel's?"

"He'll be gone after the fête and can't take it with him, so he let it fly," Zina answered icily. "Finish your *café* so I can get back to the kitchen. There's much left to be done before the guests arrive at sundown. And you'd best be ready in time, or Michie will lose all patience with you."

Beatrice took a deep breath and said, "I don't want to go to the fête."

"Is your skull thick as a pickle crock?" Zina whispered. She dropped to her knees, took

Beatrice's shoulders in her hands, and shook her. "Michie won't do anything to your pretty hide if you disobey him. It'll be Perte or Las or Kerel again that he'll punish—that's how he'll hurt you. Now get ready."

"I need to see Kerel," Beatrice said. "I'll go to the fête if I can see him."

"Have you gone mad as your *maman*? Why should he do something so dangerous?"

"Because I need to set this right."

Zina narrowed her eyes. "How?"

"Maybe we'll fly away like the grackle," Beatrice answered. She flicked open the locket as if it were a door and held it out.

Pity softened Zina's face. She pinched the locket closed in Beatrice's hand and spoke soothingly, "Your mind is cloudy, *cher*. You haven't eaten a thing in days. . . ."

Beatrice squeezed Zina's fingers hard. "Tell Kerel to meet me on the levee tonight during the fête. It will be dark at midnight. Michie and all the rest will be full of wine and I can slip away. Tell him I only need to say good-bye."

Zina yanked her hand from Beatrice's grip and stumbled back. She reached for the door, but Beatrice stopped her. "You owe me this favor. Magiic found your boy, now you do this for me in return."

"Or what?" Zina asked. Her voice trembled, but she lifted her chin defiantly.

Beatrice leaned toward her. "Or . . . or I will fix you!" For good measure she made a menacing gesture in Zina's direction.

No other threat or plea was needed. Beatrice watched with satisfaction as Zina raced past the garden, the kitchen, and on toward the smith's shop.

CHAPTER FIFTEEN

Fête

FRESHLY bathed, her dark hair glossy with beeswax pomade and arranged into fat ringlets that lay over one shoulder, Beatrice turned before the mirror in the green silk dress and layered petticoats. Her head felt naked without its *tignon*, as did her bare shoulders; and the dress's low neckline revealed the locket, which she'd not removed. Just as Tante Abeille had believed, it was a talisman, a link to Grandmère Derora. That was why Tante had searched for it in the garden and saved it for Ara.

She rummaged through a clothes trunk in the room and found an old lace shawl to cover herself. The sounds of arriving guests drifted upstairs: Michie's hearty greetings, violin music, polite exclamations over the food Tante Perte and Tante Las had spent days and days making. Zina had told her there would be roasted chickens, baguettes of wheat bread, island bananas cooked in rum, frosted cake with almonds, sweet custard frozen in a bath of salted ice that'd been specially shipped downriver from a snowy lake in the far north.

Beatrice thought of the map Michie had shown her, and the thick, black line that was Old Devil River. In her mind she followed it up the page, then off the edge and northward until it reached a place cold enough to freeze solid an entire lake.

"There is plenty of claret wine for the mamzelles, and brandy for the monsieurs," Zina said, stressing the word *plenty*. "Come morning their heads will ache." Then lowering her voice to a whisper she added, "Kerel will meet you at the levee. Say your good-byes and be quick about it. I can't think what would happen if you're caught together."

We'll say good-bye tonight, Beatrice thought, but not to each other. Her heart broke to think of how sad Tante Las and Tante Perte would be that she'd left without telling them. And how angry Zina would be at her.

Zina wasn't long gone when the key turned again in the door. Reynard's face darkened at the sight of the room in shambles, but when he caught sight of Beatrice, disbelief replaced the anger. When he spoke his voice cracked. "I knew it . . . you are my Derora come back as an angel!"

"My grandmère is long dead, Michie. Don't you remember I am Beatrice?" She spoke sweetly, as if all were forgiven.

He blinked in confusion and doddered toward her, leaning on his cane. "*Oui*, of course, but the shawl was hers . . . and that locket!" He reached out to take the jewel but swiftly drew back as if he'd been stung. When he held his hand out, blisters in the shapes of the vines, flowers, and insects etched on the locket face tipped each finger.

Beatrice touched the locket but it felt only as warm as her body.

"What game are you playing with me?" Reynard croaked. "Take the locket off and give it to me this instant! It's not yours."

"It is mine! Tante Abeille gave it to me." Beatrice pulled the lace shawl higher to cover it.

"Abeille's witchery again," Reynard said. He backed away until he stood at the threshold of the door. "I was foolish to think I was finally rid of the old crone. I should have let the dogs chase her down and been done with it.

"The fête downstairs was for your birthday, *cher*. I had wanted to show you off, see you dance a quadrille or two in that fine dress. But that crone's put some sort of spell on you, something to punish me." He smiled grimly and looked at his burned fingers. "Once the guests have gone we will speak again about that locket, and Abeille. For you, the fête is over before it begins. Happy Birthday."

And with those words he shut her in and turned the lock. Beatrice flew at it, and even though she knew it would do her no good to plead or pound on the wooden door, she did until her hands felt bruised. She had no tantrum left, and sank to the floor in defeat. Her silk skirt billowed around her, rippling like green water. She succeeded in stripping the layers of petticoats from under her skirt, but try as she might, she couldn't remove the dress itself without tearing it in half, and so left it alone. The hall clock chimed nine times.

She crept to the window and looked out at the levee and the inky stretch that was the river at night. Mawu shone at half-strength, light enough to see, dark enough to hide.

Kerel waited for her. She conjured him in her mind: every scar a star in the night sky, strong hands and shoulders working the bellows, eyes brown as warm molasses.

With little effort she found him, saw him sitting atop the levee above the river. He lay back and put his hands beneath his head. Closed his eyes and seemed to sleep.

Kerel and the smith waited atop the levee in silence. The smith pulled now and again at the stem of his pipe. Working his jaw in a rhythm, he released perfect rings of pale smoke that grew larger as they floated into the dark sky. Some large enough to encircle the half-moon before breaking apart into wisps.

From time to time Kerel glanced down at the glowing windows of the maison, and within it the silhouettes of merrymakers dancing the quadrille. He wondered which was Beatrice. He couldn't tell, though he thought he should.

Zina had told him how fine she looked dressed in her silks. "The other belles will faint with jealousy," she said. But Kerel knew Beatrice would be the most beautiful girl at the fête even if she were dressed in brown muslin. It irked him to think of her hands resting in those of some fancy young beaux. Her hands belonged in his. A whipping didn't change that. Sending him away from her didn't change that either.

"What time do you think it is?" he asked the smith. Every moment that slipped by was a wasted moment. There were too few left.

Another smoke ring swirled toward the moon. "She'll come when she can. If she can."

Kerel lay back and pinned his restless hands beneath his head. He closed his eyes and thought of Beatrice in green silk.

Beatrice startled at the sound of the clock chiming eleven. She'd held her sight on Kerel for so long it surprised her to find herself inside the maison rather than beside him on the levee. Panic seized her. Only an hour left before midnight!

She tugged at the window, putting her legs and back into it, but it rose only partway, high enough for her arms to escape, but not shoulders or head. She peered at the quiet garden below and called out, "Tante Abeille! If you can hear me, please tell me what I must do!"

She listened but there was no answer save that of the rain owl hooting in the wood, *hoo, hoo-aw!* and then the echoing answer of its mate.

"You are you own best hop—hope—help. Cast a stone." Either Tante or the bees had said those words. Either it was more riddle-speak or something simpler than that.

Crawling on hands and knees, Beatrice searched for something heavy. She found the thick base of a broken crystal candelabra beneath the bed. Standing before the window, she waited for the music and drunken merriment to grow loud, then cocked back her arm and threw the base with all her strength. A shower of glass rained down on the garden, and what remained of the crystal shattered into a thousand glittering slivers.

Beatrice wound the lace scarf around her hand. Protected, she pushed from the window frame the shards of jagged glass that remained in the lower pane until no sharp bits remained. She hiked her skirt and swung one leg over the ledge.

The brick path seemed far, much farther than when she had been fully inside. There was nothing soft to aim for if she jumped, only the path with its covering of moss, or the bramble with its claws. One hand still bore an embroidered pattern of thin, pink scars as a reminder of the morning she'd tried to push her way out of it.

But she remembered, too, how Kerel had cut her free from it. Whatever pain she felt now would be worth it to be with him. His back bore lash marks because of her, and she'd gladly bear marks for him. Wounds healed. Wounds were the price you paid for dreams, the smith had told her. Memory of struggle made visible.

Let go and push away, she told herself.

She would not think how far it was to fall, only how much closer she would be to Kerel. She swung over her other leg and sat with feet dangling high above the brick path littered with glittering glass. It seemed as dark and distant as the river. How would it feel to pitch away from the window and let the air rush past? To sprout wings and fly a path of one's own choosing? She pictured the tipsy whirling of rose beetles; the lazy gliding of butterflies; the zigzagging of Abeille's honeybees; the swift grackle. To be like them for a moment would be sublime.

But once begun there would be no turning back. Michie would not forgive her; already he was beyond reason. She couldn't allow him to decide her fate, and so she would decide for herself. The choice was hers for once. Whatever happened, at least for a moment she would fly.

She touched the locket for luck, and then slid forward until her elbows rested where her bottom had been. Her skirt bunched around her hips, and her exposed thighs prickled with gooseflesh. She closed her eyes and braced against the wall with her feet. Holding the empty window frame with one hand, she held out the other to steady herself. The locket bumped against her breastbone. "You promised to protect me, Tante Abeille," she whispered. "By all the *loa*, by Mawu, do what you promised."

Beneath her, the tangled bramble shuddered and then heaved like a mound of serpents. Every burnished leaf curled around to shield the thorny stems in a way that reminded Beatrice of the doves inside the colombier covering themselves with their wings when they slept. With each barb safely sheathed, the bower looked as deep and soft as the feather bed.

There was no sound as she pushed away and fell headlong through the air. In a wing-beat she landed atop the briar and lay among the bruised leaves and crushed berries for a moment, savoring the leap.

Inside the maison the music played on, and

voices of the belles and beaux laughed merrily. They clinked their glasses together in toast to Michie's grande fête—a harvest celebration for all to remember.

CHAPTER SIXTEEN

River

ER FEET found the way to Kerel without effort. She felt him in the world without trying, as if she were metal, and he the magnet. Perhaps in finding him once, she'd cleared the path. But he wasn't alone when she arrived atop the levee. The smith was there, and Zina with little Frey clinging to her skirt. "Your talents scare me," she said. "I came to tell them you couldn't come. Can you walk through locked doors or walls now like a ghost?"

Beatrice paid her no mind, just flew to Kerel and wrapped her arms around him. "Nothing could stop me," she said, and felt the power of those words. "I can lead us away, Kerel. Do you trust me?"

Reynard woke to the sound of banging. It pained his head, and for a moment he thought the sound came from inside his own skull. He winced and opened one eye a slit, and ran his tongue over sticky teeth.

A wedge of sunlight shone through an opening in the heavy drapes and cut a bright path across the rug. An empty wine bottle captured the light like a prism and threw points of color on the walls, as if a rainbow had shattered against it during the night.

The wine had done its job. He'd not heard anything through the fog he'd drunk himself into during the fête. Nothing had disturbed him all evening, not even a dream. Without it he might have been tempted to go upstairs and open the door to Derora's room, or Beatrice's. . . . It wasn't clear in his mind who he'd locked in it, only that he couldn't let her out until the smith's boy was gone.

He rubbed his eyes and tried to remember the evening, but most of it was lost. He'd locked the girl in her room. She'd refused to give him the locket when he asked, and it had burned him. The marks still showed on his fingers. But that was Abeille's fault, not the girl's. He regretted being harsh with her and locking her up.

The banging began anew, and he wondered who could be calling at such an early hour. He squinted up at the mantel clock but could not read it; he sighed heavily and pushed himself up from the chair he'd slept in. His joints were stiff and achy, and he limped to the front door using his cane for balance, the pointed ears of its ivory fox head handle digging into his palm. Another sharp knock sent a bolt of searing white pain through his head. Before the visitor could torture him with more rapping, he threw open the door.

The startled overseer stood with his fist poised

to knock again alongside one of the guests from the evening before—a cotton farmer who was to take the smith's boy with him. An embarrassed smile spread over the overseer's chapped lips. "It's the smith's boy, Monsieur. He's gone."

Reynard's stomach roiled uneasily. Ignoring the ache in his limbs, he climbed the stairs with great effort, and stopped for a moment outside the girl's door. He put his ear against the wooden panel and listened. All was quiet. Too quiet. He slipped the key in its slot and turned it quietly. For a moment his breath left him.

The lace curtains fluttered at the window. He moved to it as quickly as his stiff joints would allow. Broken glass crunched beneath his feet as he braced himself and peered over the sill, expecting to see Beatrice's body crumpled on the brick path below. The lace scarf she'd worn over her shoulders was snagged in the briar. It fluttered and snapped in the wind like a flag. Relief at not finding her there gave way to renewed anger.

Lifting his cane high, he slashed the ivory handle at the unbroken top pane of window glass. Glittering shards rained down over the garden like needles, like sharp, jagged seeds.

"Beatrice has run away with the boy," Reynard called out to the overseer. "Have my horse brought around, and the dogs. We'll soon find her. She will be punished. The boy will bear that punishment for her."

From the broken window he looked out beyond the garden and the alley of oaks at the gash of river, scanned the road and the levee as far as his eyes would allow. That is where she would be. It was where they all went: to the river, thinking of salvation but finding only the treachery of shifting sand, swift currents, and water too deep to know.

Beatrice, Kerel, and Zina with Frey clinging to her back traveled mostly in silence, using any word sparingly, for a spoken word added weight to the moment; weight that might tip the scales of chance away from them toward a cursed fate rather than a charmed one.

In a few short hours the sky had gone from soft rose, to melon, to butter, and now the road wasn't safe for travel. They'd been following it in a northerly direction for two reasons: south led straight to the port of Orléans and the swamps and bayous of the delta and finally to a dead end at the ocean, and the smith said north was the direction he'd gone every time he'd searched for freedom. It was the direction he'd rowed the boat when he took Derora as far away as he could. Somewhere at the head of the river there was a land of promise. "Old Papa River flows down from that land of milk and honey, and the first bright star at night shines on it. Neither cane nor cotton grows in the fields there, snow rather than ash falls from the sky in autumn, and no man owns another. Follow river or star far enough and find sweet freedom."

It might have been no more than rumor built on hope, but Beatrice clung to it. When she touched the locket and thought of Grandmère, an urgency took hold of her that assured her this was the way.

She guessed Michie had found the bedroom empty by now. He'd search the plantation first and learn that Kerel was gone, and Zina too. Her heart ached for Tante Perte and Tante Las. It would be a wrenching sorrow for them, and a terrible worry. But the smith had said he would look out for them. They were too old to run, and he was too lame. Their running days were finished.

As the day grew from the cusp of dawn toward full morning, they moved away from the road, hoping to hide in the brush and piles of driftwood beside the river until nightfall when travel would be safer.

Side by side they climbed the high ground of the earthen levee. Tall dry broom grass riffled in golden, hissing wavelets around their waists. A grackle *jeeb*ed overhead as he flew toward the river and then banked over it and returned to circle them. Kerel returned the call, and the bird spiraled down and lit on his shoulder.

A hound bayed to the south. A chorus of others bawled in answer. The grackle cocked its head and leaped away in alarm.

Beatrice stopped at the crest of the levee, struggling to catch her breath. It wasn't the climb that winded her, but panic. Clutching Kerel by the sleeve, she sank down into the broom grass and pulled him beside her. Frey began to whimper and Zina shushed him. She looked at Beatrice to do something, weave a spell of protection, or cause some harm to come to the dogs and the men chasing them.

Fear circled round Beatrice like a pack of wolves, snarling and bold. Frey wouldn't quiet; she wished Kerel hadn't begged Zina to come with them. She wished Zina hadn't believed in her power to protect them. She reached for the locket because she had nothing else, no weapon or magiic charm to turn the dogs from their scent trail.

She'd seen Tante Abeille call *loa* for help. She'd done it herself in the maison when Tante had come to her as a swarm of honeybees, but she'd had the *asson*. In her hurry to escape, she'd left it behind. But Tante said she wasn't a *loa*, wasn't a spirit. That night in the pasture, she'd cast a spell that had eaten her almost to nothingness: a stuttering voice, a tiny bee lost in a swarm.

If only to give hope to Zina and Kerel and herself, she prayed, picturing the *vevers* Abeille had drawn on the floor with flour and ash. She listened for the voices of spirits who whispered the wisdom of ten thousand ancestors into the ears of generations who remembered and honored them. The air hissed with the voice of Danbala, protector of the earth, from the dry grass and the black earth and the moving river.

The grackle screeched from a stand of trees, and Frey wailed until Zina pushed his face into her shoulder. "Two horses with the dogs," Kerel whispered. "Michie and the overseer are less than a mile from here." He pulled Beatrice and Zina to their feet and down the slope that ended at the river's edge. The bank was treacherous with sucking mud, littered with driftwood and the skeletons of fallen trees, tangled with brush and vine.

Zina and Beatrice pushed through into a pile of twisted bleached limbs. The sound of horse hooves and dogs drew nearer.

"Stay hidden!" Kerel ordered. "I'll lead them away from you." Before either could stop him, he'd sprinted to the top of the levee.

Beatrice scrambled after him and they stood together on the ridge. It mattered that they be together, she told herself. She'd not go on without him and so would stand with him.

The pair of horses broke into full gallop, and the distance that separated them from Kerel and Beatrice closed quickly. The pack of dogs swarmed round her first, nipping her heels, jumping against her legs, yanking her skirt violently. Thrown off balance, she stumbled back and fell. With the dogs still lunging and barking, she slid down the steep slope, halfway to the river.

A terrible howl pealed, loud and long, a wolf's cry. The hounds stopped so suddenly to listen that they seemed under a spell. Vicious growling and snarling followed the howl, and Kerel vaulted at the pack from the ridge. The stunned hounds broke apart and scattered. Frightened, yelping like puppies with tails between legs, they crested the levee and fled from sight.

Bitten and bruised, Beatrice struggled to her feet with Kerel's help. The torn silk dress hung round her legs, heavy with mud and water; blood streaked her elbows and arms. Michie Reynard and the overseer, both still horse-mounted, looked down at them in each other's arms. Michie's face looked like roiling smoke clouds, gray and angry, with eyes ablaze. He twitched with a rage that surely burned all words to cinder in his throat, because he spoke none.

"Climb up to us, girl," the overseer called. "It

will be worse for the boy and his sister if I come down there."

Beatrice felt all heat leave her body; rainwater pumped through her veins; her bones felt as hollow as a bird's. The overseer dismounted and stood with hands on hips. "Last chance. Come by yourselves or I'll bring my riding crop down and give your backs a good striping."

Reynard held up Tante Abeille's *asson* in his hand. "Where is that old crone Abeille hiding? She put you up to this. Has she abandoned you to your fate?" He slid from his saddle and joined the overseer.

Beatrice and Kerel backed to the very edge of the narrow sand beach, to the place where all fell away into the river's current. Beatrice imagined water closing over, her mouth filling with water and silt, and the thought held her poised on the balance.

"Go and get them," Reynard snapped at the overseer.

Beatrice found her voice, though it trembled.

"I will jump into the river before I let you take me. I will become a spirit like my grandmère Derora, and I vow to haunt you until your death. You'll beg me to leave you alone."

Reynard gaped at her, brimming with outrage. He sneered for the overseer's sake, but she heard a waver in his voice, a high-pitched note of fear. "Derora has no power over me, no more than is in this witch's tool." He lifted the *asson* over his head and shook it until the snake bones hissed inside it, as if they'd found life again.

The overseer laughed and began to make his way down the slope. A slight wind stirred the broom grass around his hips. Kerel's grackle screeched and flew above them. He darted at the horses' faces and sent them dancing askitter.

Intense heat prickled Beatrice's neck, as if a thin, hot wire encircled it, and she remembered the burns put on Michie's fingers when he'd tried to take the locket. She grabbed Kerel's hand, and the heat raced through her shoulder and arm and into their hands clenched together. Kerel caught his breath, and she could only imagine that the heat now traveled up his arm and into his shoulder. She squeezed his hand and turned to him, sorry that she'd let him come with her. Sorry, too, for Zina and Frey, both weeping with fright.

"Together?" Kerel asked without hesitation, his voice so certain it broke her heart. She understood. He would cast his fate with hers. He would leap with her; choose to fight the river rather than wait for what would come and be handed to them.

The wind picked up speed. It blew with force enough to snatch the overseer's hat from his head and send it tumbling brim over crown into the river. His clothes snapped. It took effort to put one foot before the other. He leaned forward, pushing into the gusts with resolve. Reynard searched the sky, wary, and dropped the *asson* in the riffling grass, to take shelter between the horses.

Immediately the wind died. The overseer, having suddenly lost his leverage against the gale,

pitched forward. The momentum sent him careen-
ing, arms and legs spinning, hands clawing the air
for purchase or balance where there was none, and
with a mighty splash he hit the water. He surfaced
once, sputtering and gasping, and then the current
swept him up and pulled him down. When he surfaced again he was far away, near the deep middle
channel, choking and spewing water. And then they
lost sight of him.

Beatrice felt the river's cold fingers pulling
at her own heels, reaching up from the silty depths
to the edge of the dropaway, loosening the sand
beneath their feet. And high above them on the
ridge, Reynard cowered between the horses, unable
to put himself again in the saddle because his legs
could not do the work of lifting him up. Beatrice
sensed his frustration. Grim was the look he fixed on
her, defiant and sorrowful. His green eyes held hers
and she held his in return. She did not need to look
away, for there she saw herself reflected, as in those
tall windows that mirrored the garden.

She led Kerel onto firmer ground and gestured for Zina to join him. Slowly she climbed the levee a final time. To stand before Reynard without fear, without shackles, with eyes clear enough to see him truly, and have him see her.

"I am not your slave," she said. "Kerel is not your slave, nor Zina or Frey. You cannot keep us."

He steadied himself against the flank of his horse. The fold of skin beneath his chin quivered, but his voice did not betray him. "I can and will keep what belongs to me. Tell me what you are, then, if not slaves of Rillieux Plantation, born to a slave mother."

"A slave who was your own daughter," Beatrice interrupted, her voice catching. "Grandpère, if you enslave your own blood you enslave yourself. Free us all. Let us go." She took the silver chain from beneath her bodice and rolled it between her fingers. "Grandmère will never let you rest until you do."

He slumped against the horse, clinging to the

saddle strap. "You promised never to leave me. If you keep your promise, I will let the boy and his sister go."

"And Perte and Las? And the smith?"

Reynard stiffened and glared at her. "All those for the price of one girl?"

"One who is a seer, who sees who you are and knows the same red river runs from you to me. I will keep my promise."

"One who drives a hard bargain," he admitted. "Call the others up from the river and we will finish this. They'll not get far without papers to show, and it will take all of you to lift me to my saddle so that I can ride back and get them."

She knew Kerel wouldn't want to go without her. But he and Zina would find their way north and start a life.

She turned and waved Kerel and Zina toward her, smiling to show all danger had passed. A bargain had been reached.

But for just one second, at that same moment,

Beatrice heard whistling, and then day met twilight as her head burst with bright pain. She staggered and dropped to her knees in the grass, and saw in the small, quickly dimming circle of her wakeful mind an image: the ivory fox head and Reynard's hand gripping the ebony shaft of his cane as he swung it out from behind his back. Her vision from the garden.

But this was no dream or wisp of the garden. This was real.

"*Foolish* lapin *trust old man* krokodi. . . ." Tante Abeille had warned her.

Through the dark veil she heard Kerel howling, and Frey shrieking, but she did nothing, for she could do nothing but lie in the dry grass and search for a ray of light to guide her back to them. The light was a seed in the blank gray twilight, and a woman held it in her palm like a pearl and chanted:

> *"Warm beneath the soil I dreamed*
> *in winter; a sleeping seed: breathless, still,*

> *with bitterness on my tongue.*
> *Like spring, awoke to moonlit hope,*
> *with nectar on my lips,*
> *And wings where there were none."*

"*Grandmère!*" Beatrice called, holding her hands out. The woman smiled but did not take them. Beatrice found her open hands filled with pearls of light that fell from the moon like rain, or tears. They lit the path that brought her back to Kerel, and the world.

Kerel struggled to drag her out of reach of Reynard's cane, pleading for her to help him. Her head still swam, but she gathered her wits enough to crawl, surprised that only a few minutes had passed. Reynard could not follow them easily through the long grass; even with his cane, the grass caught his feet in a tangle and worked to trip him. But he would not so easily give up what he owned, and so yanked the horse along to help him balance while he swung the cane over the grass like a scythe.

"Leave her," he bellowed at Kerel, his breath wheezing. "Take your sister and run while you can. Go where you will; I won't follow you."

Kerel answered with a shrill whinny that stopped Reynard's horse in its tracks. By luck of being on hands and knees, or perhaps by finder's talent, Beatrice came upon the *asson* that Reynard had dropped. She rose to her knees, swaying, frightened and righteous, and shook it at him, hoping to call the wind again, a storm, a flood of rain, lightning.

What came was a ponderous quiet and the strangely familiar odor of vinegar and bitter almond rising up in the heavy air, so sharp it stung her nose, so strong it drowned the smell of boiling syrup. With it came the sound of bees.

They streamed up from the burned fields of stubbled cane like long dark fingers. They massed together and pushed upward on the levee slope to swarm around Beatrice and Kerel like a whirlwind. Tante Abeille's laughter crackled across the thrumming.

For a moment Beatrice listened to the droning. She closed her eyes; it sounded like words chanted or sung.

Kerel put his mouth to her ear and spoke the vibrant words so that she could understand them. "Without belief, no strength."

The cloud of honeybees landed one atop another, on her shoulders and his. She wasn't afraid, for she remembered holding them in her hands like warm raisins without harm. But Kerel cringed and shuddered, near to bolting. Before he could run, she stood and wrapped her arms around him. "Together. Without you I won't know what they're saying."

The ripe smell of vinegar grew more pungent, and the bees strummed louder. More of them surged up the slope, pushing Zina and Frey ahead of them. They covered necks and arms and hands. They clung to clothes like patches of sticky brown burrs. The honeybees covered Beatrice from collar to skirt hem in a robe of brown velvet bodies. They bejeweled her hair like dusty nuggets of gold and jet. They stroked her with their feelers and offered her tastes of honey and bits of pollen.

Kerel looked as if he wore a fine velvet cap. Zina and Frey peered from a cloak with two hoods.

Reynard swiped at the grass and air equally as he moved closer, wrestling the skittish horse. He reached his hand out toward Beatrice. "I am your grandpère. What family but me do you have?"

"Kerel. Tante Las and Tante Perte. By love's measure they are my only family. And never again will I call you Grandpère. We are bound by blood, not love."

At that, Reynard swung his cane at her through the flying bees.

They shot at him like a storm of arrows, piercing him with venomous barbs. Abeille's voice cackled from among the swirl, and cried out, "Run if you will, old man, run if you can. You will not outrun the curse you've worked upon yourself!"

Reynard slung at the bees, desperate and enraged.

Clawing and slapping at his face and his neck, he scrambled. Crawling on hands and knees as Beatrice had, he wanted only to escape the swarm, to be left alone with his wounds. But there was no shelter on the levee, no comfort, no walls to protect or hide him. He reached for the horse's reins. Wild-eyed now, the horse tossed its head and reared. Reynard tottered and fell as it bolted down the slope, and ran away south down the river road.

The bees blanketed Beatrice and Kerel and Zina and Frey entirely, until nothing showed but their faces. Then with a great screaming of wings and whipping wind, the grass bowed to the ground around them, and the honeybees lifted them into the air and swept them up and away across the churning river.

CHAPTER SEVENTEEN

Honey

EATRICE settled down on the front step in a splash of golden sunshine. It was warm for a northern spring, though she'd only seen one other. She raised her cup to her lips and sipped before setting it beside her. In Louisián the cane would be shoulder high by now and the flowers just unfurling in the *jardin de fleurs*. It surprised her to miss the garden, but she did. More than a year had passed, and she thought of it still.

honeybees down in sugar country, she told me, and her sister would be coming to stay. When I saw the smoke in the chimney, I came thinking that's who I'd find. Miss Derora was a healer, and a midwife. Eased into the world nearly every child around here. Me included."

He took them to her grave, her true grave and resting place, not a slave's plot full of old sorrows. It was marked with a simple cross and the name, *Derora*. No last name.

There Ezer told them the story she had told him: Miss Derora had escaped slavery with her sister's help. Some brew of bitter herbs they cooked up all but killed her, and after she was boxed and nearly buried, her sister returned in darkness to wake her. Another brew, sweeter than the first, woke her and set her free.

Burials and unburials, Beatrice remembered Abeille saying. There was much to learn about the old ways. *Wanga* had its place if you didn't mind the price of it. All was balance.

Along with the signs that had lead them north, the *asson* rested on the mantel and a pot for Grandmère to rest in when her spirit visited, and candles of beeswax to sweeten the air with the breath of honeybees.

Kerel prenticed himself to a blacksmith in Cairo. Ezer sometimes looked after Frey for Zina when she helped Beatrice with the hives, especially at harvest when there was much to do.

Contentedly, Beatrice hugged her knees to her chest, basking in the warmth of the step and the light on her face. She was a beekeeper and a seer, a student of Grandmère and Tante Abeille: sister-twins, two halves of one soul together again at last. There was much to learn, much to teach.

"A bird builds its nest one straw at a time," Tante Abeille liked to say when Beatrice felt impatient to know everything in a day.

As she did on some mornings, Beatrice closed her eyes and pushed out toward the bright white-ness behind her eyelids. Time and space closed in around her like cool liquid or moist air. She shot through it toward a familiar place, Rillieux Plantation. Mostly because she longed to see the garden again, and Tante Perte and Tante Las. And Kerel would want news of the blacksmith if she could get it.

She hovered for a moment over the garden. Magnolia and honeysuckle perfumed the air. A few brave blossoms of azalea and plumbago held their heads above the bramble, but runners and shoots and generations of new briar seedlings had smothered nearly everything else, for the birds had dropped ten thousand juice-stained seeds to sprout in the dangerous, glass-ruined soil. But the old bramble sang with the music of beetle wings and bee's work and rustling leaves. It pressed burred canes against the library windows and scratched at the glass when the wind blew.

Beatrice slipped past the rotted edge of one tall window as easily as a draft of air moves through a net veil. Reynard sat before the empty hearth in a chair fitted with two wooden wheels that reminded her of the mule-driven turn wheel on the mill. A knitted shawl covered his withered legs, and his one good hand twitched in his lap with a life all its own. As always she circled around until she saw his face. The right side drooped worse than ever, like beeswax that'd been left too long near a fire.

"*Hello, vieux,*" she said, pushing the words into his ear with her mind's voice.

His hand shook more violently at the sound of her voice. "*Go away if you've come to punish me.*" His mind's voice was not old to match his body, but young and full of vinegar.

"*'Old man' is what you are. And if I go, who will you talk to? The fits have made your poor tongue silent. Everyone thinks you are already dead, but you are trapped inside your head. I am the only one who knows, and all you have left.*"

Reynard shook in the chair until Beatrice worried that he would fall from it. "*I am here alone! You aren't real. You're less than smoke; you are my own madness.*

Or a ghost come to haunt me, my granddaughter's ghost here to torture me."

Beatrice sighed. *"You torture yourself, vieux. That's my grandmère's tignon you have tied around your neck."*

"A rag I found on the briar, and it serves to keep my neck warm. Nothing to do with you or her, who left me alone to grow old and rot."

His eyes brimmed. Grunting with the effort, he raised his good arm to cover his face. It had grown too heavy for him, and it moved in ways he didn't ask it to, as if it were constantly stirring a pot, the fingers rolling beads of dough. In defeat, he closed his lids and let the tears trickle down his cheeks and neck and soak the ragged *tignon*. Drops of sorrow slipped inside the corner of his mouth, and his head bobbed as he worked to spit them out.

"You've caused so many tears; it's high time you had a taste of them for yourself," she said.

"If you are going to bring me bitterness when you visit, you could at least call me Grandpère. A small thing, a grain of sugar to ease the harsh medicine you feed me."

"I'll never call you that. But I will come from time to time."

"Why does Derora come no more?"

"Grandmère has no more link to you or this place," she answered gently. "I am free. Her sister is gone. I can come because we are blood linked. And because you freed Tante Perte and Tante Las as I asked you, if not the smith."

"I had papers drawn that name you as my heir. Come here and free the smith yourself."

"To trust you again would truly make me a foolish lapin. Non, I won't come, but I thank you for letting Perte and Las stay. They're too old to travel. The kitchen is all they know, and they're used to caring for you."

"Visit again tomorrow then," he demanded, desperate. "You will come every day and we will talk like we once did about the things we talked of then. You can tell the stories now, and stay as long as I need you."

She answered, "I will come again, but only when I choose, and I will leave when I choose. All your choices have been made, and they have brought you to this. You cannot demand anything. It is your curse, your malédiction, to die *alone, helpless, without voice. But you are not dead yet, and so it's not too late for your soul.*

"*Au revoir, vieux.*"

Reynard's low-pitched howl followed her as she slipped from the library and pulsed away from him on a current of blinding light.

Returned to herself and the cottage, she opened her eyes and breathed deep, savoring the memory of honeysuckle and magnolia. A chain vine cloaked the sunniest side of the cottage with fiery blooms in summer. Its scent reminded her of honeysuckle, and the honeybees loved it. On warm days they gathered on it to drink nectar and sing to her, though only Kerel understood their words. Her honeybees skimmed the wildflower fields or hovered around the blossoms of the rambling white rose that crowned an arbor Kerel had built.

The oldest bee in the hive was Abeille, but she rarely flew farther than hive to house. When days were warm she spent hours sitting on Beatrice's shoulder. The *wanga* curse had taken its price from her as she'd known it would, but she seemed content with it: to spend her last days with two true wings on her back. Beatrice went with her at night to visit the row of hives that perched along the fence rail. If Kerel was there he told her what the worker bees said of the happenings on nearby farms and in the town of Cairo.

True enough: one or two people swore they had been out to the cottage to buy honey and had seen the woman Beatrice dancing amid a swirling storm of honeybees. "Her feet scarcely touched the ground," they whispered. "Her eyes were open wide."

But no matter, the townsfolk bought every drop of honey she and Zina ever brought to market. Some gave up buying sugar altogether.

"By magic charm or miracle, it's the best honey in creation," they agreed. "There's nothing sweeter."

But Beatrice knew true sweetness. On her tongue it tasted like freedom.

Glossary

Arpent *(ahr-pahng)*: An acre of land.

Asson *(ah-sohn)*: Sacred rattle used during vodou ceremonies by an initiated priest or priestess.

Ayida-Wedo *(ah-yee-dah way-do)*: One of the oldest and wisest female spirits in the vodou religion, who is wife of Dambala, and referred to sometimes as "mother."

Baka *(bah-kah)*: An evil spirit created by black magic that devours the life spirit of its victim (vodou).

Beignet *(ben-yey)*: Fried pastry similar to a pillow-shaped doughnut.

Bonjou *(bon-shu)*: Hello.

Cher *(sha)*: My dear.

Dambala *(dom-bah-lah)*: The vodou creator spirit represented by a serpent, married to *Ayida-Wedo*, and sometimes referred to as "father."

Diab *(dee-ahb)*: A devil (vodou).

Dromi l'mort *(drom-eh lah-mor)*: To sleep like the dead.

Grande maison *(grahngd may-zong)*: The big house or master's quarters.

Hibou *(ee-boo)*: Owl.

Jardin de fleurs *(shar-dang d-fler)*: Flower garden.

Krokodi *(krock-oh-dee)*: Crocodile.

Lapin *(lah-pang)*: Rabbit/hare.

Loa *(l-wah)*: Supernatural, immortal vodou spirits who oversee different parts of the natural world and human experiences.

Magiic: Magic.

Mais oui *(may wee)*: Oh, yes!

Mal *(mahl)*: Something evil, a sickness.

Maman *(mah-mahng)*: Mother; also the largest of three drums used in vodou rituals.

Mambo *(mahm-bow)*: A fully initiated priestess of vodou.

Marasa *(mah-rah-sah)*: The sacred twins, believed to have supernatural powers.

Mawu *(mah-woo)*: An African (Fon) creator spirit represented by the moon, who is the goddess of joy, fertility, and rest.

Merci *(mair-see)*: Thank you.

Mo chagren *(moh shah-grah)*: I'm sorry.

Papa Legba *(pah-pah leg-bah)*: A powerful vodou spirit who guards the gate or opening between the spirit world and the human world.

Piti *(peh-tee)*: Child.

Qualité *(kah-li-tay)*: Of good blood, upstanding and favorable character.

Sa ena? *(sah enah)*: What's wrong?

Sang mêlé *(sahng may-leh)*: Literally, "mixed blood," used to describe someone of racially mixed heritage.

Tante *(tahnt)*: Aunt.

Tignon *(tee-yahng)*: Head scarf worn by Creole women.

Vever *(vay-vay)*: A drawn set of ornate symbols that represents a particular *loa*; comparable to a written name and used as an invocation during a ceremony.

Vieux (*vi-ew*): Old man.

Wanga (*wahn-gah*): A spell or curse (vodou).

Zombie (*zom-bee*): A body without a soul that's been raised from the dead by vodou black magic.

Zut! (*zuht*): An expression of exasperation or distaste.